T0273686

DREAMS OF A ROBOT DANCING BEE

DREAMS OF A ROBOT DANCING BEE

44 STORIES BY

JAMES TATE

WAVE BOOKS

SEATTLE / NEW YORK

Published by Wave Books www.wavepoetry.com

ISBN 978-1-933517-35-3

Originally Published by Verse Press

All Wave Books titles are distributed to the trade by
Consortium Book Sales and Distribution
Phone: 800-283-3572 / SAN 631-760X

The following stories appeared previously and are reprinted by permission of the author: "Little Man, What Now?" and "Hedges, by Sam D'Amico" in *Columbia*. "Mush" in *Franck* (Paris). "Suite 1306" in *The Missouri Review*. "Raven of Dawn" in *New Letters*. "The Thistle" and "Welcome Signs" in *The North American Review*. "Dear Customer," and "The New Teacher" in *Ploughshares*. "A Cloud of Dust" and "Dreams of a Robot Dancing Bee" in *Sonora Review*. "Eating Out of Mousetraps" and "Robes" in *Denver Quarterly*. "At the Ritz" and "Vacation" in *Boulevard*. "Running for Your Life" in *Georgia Review*. "Pie" and "My Burden" in *The Illinois Review*. "The Stove" and "What It Is" in *Black Warrior Review*. "TV" in *Michigan Quarterly*. "Pie," "Dear Customer," "The Torque-Master of Advanced Video," "The Examination," and "The Invisible Twins" in *Denver Quarterly*.

The following stories © 1999 by the University of Michigan Press and reprinted by permission of the publisher: "At the Ritz," "What It Is," "Despair Ice Cream," "Dreams of a Robot Dancing Bee," "Vacation," "A Cloud of Dust," "The Thistle," "Pie," and "Dear Customer."

The Library of Congress has cataloged the
Verse Press hardcover edition as follows:
Tate, James, 1943–
Dreams of a robot dancing bee : stories / by James Tate.
p. cm.
ISBN 0-9703672-5-2 (hardcover)
I. Title.
PS3570.A8 D74 2002
813′.54—dc21
2001006107

Printed in the United States of America

9 8 7 6 5 4 3 2 1

FIRST PAPERBACK EDITION

CONTENTS

DREAMS OF A ROBOT DANCING BEE

THE THISTLE

I'm sitting there in my den reading an article about the devastating effects of cyberphilia on the contemporary American family, or what's left of it. Cyberphilia, in case you don't know by now, is the compulsion to program and operate a computer, in preference to all other activities (I don't own a computer, I am a cyberphobiac). Anyway, I am still interested in this article, I am gloating away at the verification of my original predictions, when in comes Eileen barking at me: "Paul, would you please get off your duff and go out to the driveway and cut down that damned thistle. If I've asked you once I've asked you a dozen times to cut it down."

"What's that thistle done to you?" I reply, as I have probably replied at each of her requests all week. I am not allowed to read an article in peace in my study. I have worked for years so that I might be allowed to read an article all the way through to the end on a hot and muggy Saturday afternoon. But no, when Eileen wants a thistle removed from the driveway, then all else must be foresworn and her command obeyed or I will get no peace, the pleasure of reading about the domestic tragedies of the cyberphiliacs has been shattered. Eileen does not take my pleasure very seriously. She doesn't understand my admittedly rather desperate need to be right about *something*. "Eileen," I said, in one last doomed attempt to defeat the General, "it's not as though that thistle's going to tear the fender off the car ... Alright, alright, I'm going ..."

So I put down my magazine, deprived of even getting to the juicy statistics and a few sample horror stories of children who have not spoken to their parents for years, husbands who have lost all sex drive, etc. The kind of stories that make me feel good about myself, that tell me I was right to never learn what that particular revolution was all about. No, instead I must go out into the sweltering, stifling shed; hunt around among oily rags and hyperactive wasps and hornets for the hedge-clippers—all this so that I can destroy the national emblem of Scotland. But I am by now something of an obedient cur. Oh, it's a well-enough adjusted thralldom I endure.

So I locate the clippers, beneath, as I predicted, the mountain of oily rags, and I am buzzed and tormented by every known species of wasp and hornet, and, since I am allergic to all of their venoms, I am justified in calling this a life-threatening tour of duty. One sting and it's all yours, Eileen: years of National Geographics, all yours, a treasure. The six boxes of travel brochures, all yours. So much rubbish to prove one's been here, been around. And all of it undoubtedly in the dust-bin before my bones have stopped shaking. All the beloved rubbish, interchangeable with the next guy's. Why the hell not leave well-enough alone, let me go on reading about the smart guy who starved to death in front of his microelectric doo-da. No, no, no, never could it be so.

On Saturdays, Eileen likes nothing better than to issue orders for me to kill things, or be killed: *Those wasp nests on the shutters, kill them. The skunk got in the garbage again last night: find him and kill him (or get sprayed by him). Or better yet, get bitten by him, undergo a series of hideous rabies shots—since you mortally fear needles—Get up Paul, put down your beloved magazine, Paul, get out there on the frontline, Paul. Risk your life, Paul. Whatever you do, Paul, don't let yourself get caught in a situation where you might feel comfortable, safe, or even right in one of your predictions.*

So now, here at last, I stand before this stately, decorous *Onopordum acanthium.* It is approximately three-and-a-half feet in height and, I regret to report, in magnificent bloom. This is, I realize even more emphatically, a totally senseless execution. I would have preferred she had ordered me to cross the street and cut the throat of the neighbor's dog. Yes, I could have accepted that order since the creature has an apparently incurable tendency to howl at the moon and kept us awake most of last night (most of the past six years is more accurate). But this thistle is a thing of almost breathtaking beauty, given to us by chance, and since Chance seems to be our new God, why am I now ordered to risk incurring the wrath of our new—and, most likely, extremely terrible and cruel when irritated—God? Eileen's whim. *Paul, go cut down that thistle by the driveway.* "Why, my dear? Why should I cut down the thistle?" *Because I said so, Paul. Now, do it before I get mad!*

It is beginning to rain. As I stand here before this delicate, purple flower with orders to kill, storm clouds are moiling up out of the hills. I can feel the barometric pressure dropping by the minute, and it is beginning to make me feel light-headed. These summer electric storms have been having this effect on me the past couple of years. I have never actually fainted, but I feel as if I am going to, and it is quite unpleasant. Perhaps I shall faint and never wake up again. Then Eileen would have to do all the murdering herself. Would she feel differently then? Perhaps that would be good for her. After her first bloodshed, say, pouring snail-poison down a mole-hole, and all the little blind star-nosed babies emerge gasping for air, perhaps, she'd give it up and become the patron saint of pests and varmints and thistles.

Now lightning is flashing and there is that deep rumbling that always precedes a real bang-up summer fury. I enjoyed them as a child, felt brave as I comforted my mother, who was terrified out of her mind by lightning. (That's where my child's imagination came up short: I thought it wouldn't strike *me*.) But now, add another entry to my slowly growing list of ... well, I won't call them phobias, but things-that-fail-to-please-me. At the moment, I feel I may just keel over and be done with it, not have the slain thistle on my list of crimes when I show up at Chanceville.

However, if I make it back to the house and report to the General that her bidding had not been done, she may very well kill me, or at least make certain I never again pick up that magazine and find out just how awful other, more modern people's lives have become. I'll take my chances. I'll tell her it had to stop somewhere, all this killing. And I've taken my stand, finally, with this thistle.

WHAT IT IS

I was going to cry so I left the room and hid myself. A butterfly had let itself into the house and was breathing all the air fit to breathe. Janis was knitting me a sweater so I wouldn't freeze. Polly had just dismembered her anatomically correct doll. The dog was thinking about last summer, alternately bitter and amused.

I said to myself, *So what have you got to be happy about?* I was in the attic with a 3000 year old Etruscan coin. *At least you didn't wholly reveal yourself,* I said. I didn't have the slightest idea what I meant when I said that. So I repeated it in a slightly revised version: *At least you didn't totally reveal yourself,* I said, still perplexed, but also fascinated. I was arriving at a language that was really my own; that is, it no longer concerned others, it no longer sought common ground. I was cutting the anchor.

Polly walked in without knocking: "There's a package from UPS," she announced.

"Well, I'm not expecting anything," I replied.

She stood there frowning. And then, uninvited, she sat down on a little rug. That rug had always been a mystery to me. No one knew where it came from and yet it had always been there. We never talked of moving it or throwing it out. I don't think it had ever been washed. Someone should at least shake it from time to time, expose it to some air.

WHAT IT IS

"You're not even curious," she said.

"About what?" The coin was burning a hole in my hand. And the rug was beginning to move, imperceptibly, but I was fairly sure it was beginning to move, or at least thinking of moving.

"The package," she said. "You probably ordered something late at night like you always do and now you've forgotten. It'll be a surprise. I like it when you do that because you always order the most useless things."

"Your pigtails are starting to crumble," I said. "Is there anywhere in the world you would rather live?" I inquired. It was a sincere question, the last one I had in stock.

"What's wrong with this?" she replied, and looked around the attic as if we might make do.

"I guess there are shortages everywhere," I said. "People find ways. I don't know how they do it but they do. Either that or . . ." and I stopped. "Children deserve better," I said. "But they're always getting by with less. I only pity the rich. They're dying faster than the rest of us."

When I get in these moods, Polly's the one I don't have to explain myself to, she just glides with me along the bottom, papa sting-ray and his daughter, sad, loving, beautiful—whatever it is, she just glides with me.

"Are you ever coming down again?" she asked, without petulance or pressure, just a point of information.

"Not until I'm very, very old. I have to get wise before I can come down, and I'm afraid that is going to take a very long time. It will be worth it," I said, "you'll see."

"Daddy," she said, "I think you know something already."

THE NORTH COUNTRY

"As a rule," Nona Kuncio was fond of saying, "it doesn't take a Sigmund Freud to understand why a man wants to catch a rainbow trout." She and her husband Jerry bought the camp four years ago after Jerry's logging accident. Nona kept an eye on all the guests. Most of them she had figured out within a few hours of their arrival. But Jerry liked everyone, even Mr. Lunceford.

When Lunceford registered, Nona knew by instinct the man was not a sportsman. The home address he listed on the slip was a full two-days' drive from there. People came from all over the country, but they came for the fishing. Mr. Lunceford checked-in without so much as a hook and a piece of string. Nona told Jerry: "He looks like some kind of CIA agent trying to pass himself off as a librarian."

Jerry offered to loan him some of his tackle.

"That's very kind of you, Mr. Kuncio. I may take you up on it, but for now the peace and quiet are all that I need."

"Just call me Jerry. Lake Umbagog is known all over for its great rainbow fishing. If you change your mind, just let me know."

Nona told Jerry, partially just to get a rise out of him: "Maybe he's on the lam. You should check the wanted posters when you go to the post office this afternoon." He was so naive when it came to these things.

"Mr. Lunceford? He looks about as much like a criminal as I look like Paul Newman. Really, Nona, you've got some kind of imagination."

"The perfect disguise," Nona retorted.

Lunceford didn't leave his cabin the whole first day. He opened his door several times to throw balls of bread to the ducks bobbing on the windy waters a few feet away. Nona now knew his type and put him out of mind.

Jerry took him at his word, that he just needed a little peace and quiet, but he also worried about Lunceford's comfort. The cabins were furnished only spartanly, and the nearest store for provisions was six miles away. Mr. Lunceford didn't appear to have brought much with him. Jerry wanted to tell his guest where he could find certain necessities in the area, but at the same time he didn't want to disturb Mr. Lunceford's privacy. It was a small dilemma.

"What's the big deal?" Nona said. "If he came here to starve to death, that's his business, as long as he's paid in full." Nona liked to exaggerate her callousness at times just to shock her husband who took his guests' happiness to heart. He was personally hurt if their vacation at Lake Umbagog was in any way less than perfect. He even took responsibility for the weather. And if they didn't catch any fish for the first couple of times out on their own, then he would drop what he was doing and go out with them. This annoyed Nona to no end when he was supposed to be helping her, but it is also why she married him. He cared about everybody.

Jerry felt a little ashamed when he caught himself stealing

glances toward Lunceford's cabin windows as he pretended to see to some chore or another. Lunceford had placed a towel over the window that faced the cabin nearest him. Maybe he was a CIA agent, maybe he was a criminal. But, still, he was a human being too. When Lunceford caught Jerry obviously looking toward his undraped kitchen window, he waved him in.

"I didn't want to disturb you, but I was worried . . ."

"Nonsense, come in. I could use a little company."

Mr. Lunceford put on a pot of coffee and seemed pleased that the owner of the cabin had consented to join him.

"It's a lovely place you have here," he said to Jerry, "I envy you."

"I was born just twenty miles from here," Jerry said. "I never wanted to live anyplace else."

"I can see why." Lunceford poured steaming coffee. "And your wife, is she from around here too?"

"Nona? No, she's from Philadelphia, a city girl. She still has family there, I guess they think she's crazy for living like this, you know how in-laws are—nothing's ever good enough for their little girl . . ."

"Have they ever visited you here?"

"Once, the first year. They were lost for three days just trying to find us. It was pretty funny. They had read somewhere that there was a high population density of black bears around here, and they were afraid to walk from the lodge to their cabin after dark. I had to escort them with a flashlight and a rifle. They insisted on the rifle."

Lunceford appreciated the humor of the situation and smiled.

Jerry felt him loosening up and felt a kinship with the man, though, most likely, they had little or nothing in common. The two men blew on their coffee and took first sips. Jerry wanted to ask Lunceford about himself, but the man looked wholly contained right where he was, without family, without history, without even a fishing pole. Maybe he was CIA. There were missiles buried in the hills and mountains near Lake Umbagog. And, though he had never thought about it before, it occurred to him now that that might attract enemy agents, and therefore ... All his life he had felt safe in this far northern corner. He didn't even own a television set, and those locals who did only got one channel faintly a few weeks in the fall.

"And I don't suppose you can get away from here to visit them in Philadelphia?"

"What? Oh no. We're open twelve months a year; hunters in the fall, cross-country skiers in the winter. It's pretty much a full-time job." The water was splashing on the rocks just feet away from the cabin door, and the sound lulled the men into easy silences. Jerry noticed a tape-machine beside the bed in the other room. He also saw what he took to be a large stack of computer print-outs on the little desk in the bedroom. Here, in the north country, they were as common as Dead Sea Scrolls, which is to say, Jerry had never seen computer print-outs before. He just imagined that that was what they must be. He finished his coffee in several gulps and thanked Lunceford for the conversation, "If you change your mind about the fishing, I'd be glad to take you out."

"I'll keep it in mind," Lunceford replied, walking him to the door.

Nona now saw her chance to play Jerry along. He always wanted everybody to be so nice. "Sure," she said, "he's probably got ultra-sensitive listening devices planted all over the campground by now." Then she put her finger to her lips. "Outside," she whispered, and motioned for Jerry to tiptoe. "Now listen to me," she said once they were safe under the birches, "There's that Hungarian fellow in cabin 8. Sure, he fishes. Of course he fishes. He's smarter than this Lunceford character. Lunceford's calling attention to himself by *not* fishing. Americans are the stupidest. The Hungarian acts like he's on a holiday, walks around in the open greeting everybody ever so politely. But this Lunceford is an embarrassment to our National Security."

Jerry looked worried now, Nona was right. If he could tell that Lunceford was an agent, then surely everyone else could tell. He thought it over for a moment.

"Do you think I should say something to Mr. Lunceford? I don't want anybody getting hurt here."

"Protect yourself, Honey, that's my advice. These guys think nothing of slitting the throats of innocent people. They play for high stakes. They can kill you 97 ways before Sunday and you'll never know what happened. They always make it look like an accident, and the government hushes everybody up. Your name won't even appear in the obituaries." She had him going now. Jerry looked out on the lake and wondered if even the ducks were bugged or concealing some kind of explosives.

THE NORTH COUNTRY

For the first time in years, Jerry slept poorly that night. The pure mountain air and his own hard work usually knocked him out within a matter of minutes of putting his head to the pillow. This night, however, long after he should have been sawing logs, he thought he heard voices. He rolled over to snuggle up to Nona, but she wasn't there. It was very late. Her absence frightened him. He called her name several times and fumbled in the darkness for the lamp-switch. A loon called in the distance, and he wondered if he was dreaming. There hadn't been loons on Lake Umbagog for several years, since the first year. But, then, distinctly, eerily, it called again.

He heard Nona talking softly from the kitchen: "Yes, I think so, I think that might be possible. He's taken the bait, isn't that a scream? I'll work on him. I can't give you a date. It's too early. Perhaps we'll be home before the holidays. I'll see what I can do. I love you, too." Nona jumped when she saw Jerry standing in the doorway. "What are you doing up?" she asked. "Who was that? Who were you talking to at this hour?" He was almost angry.

"It's only eleven o'clock. That was my mother. She just wanted to know how we were doing. Now go back to bed, nothing's wrong. I'll be in bed in a few minutes." Instinctively, though half-asleep, Jerry went to the window facing Mr. Lunceford's cabin. All the lights were on. And over by cabin #8 someone was crouched with a tiny flashlight, digging in an over-turned trash barrel.

The next morning, his last in the north country, Mr. Lunceford looked out his front window and saw Jerry Kuncio working on a motor down on the dock. He had never been much of a fisherman, but had been touched by Jerry's offer to take him out personally. So, he finished dressing and made his way down to the dock.

"Beautiful morning!" he shouted.

Jerry looked at his watch automatically. It was still morning, though he had been up since five. The best fishing was long over. "I slept like a baby," Mr. Lunceford continued as Jerry finished tightening up a new fuel hose.

"I wish I could say the same," Jerry replied. "I had the damnedest dreams, couldn't sleep most of the night."

"Sorry to hear that," Mr. Lunceford replied, himself a frequent insomniac. Somehow he hadn't thought the working folk of the north country would suffer from what he thought was the urban dweller's disease.

"Does your offer still stand, I mean about the fishing?"

Jerry looked up from the motor and gave Lunceford a long gaze. Maybe Nona's mother had sent him, she was capable of doing something like that. They'd never been happy about her marriage to him. He'd thought that they would finally get off his back when he made a go of the lodge and cabins, but he was wrong, as usual. Now they were afraid she was really entrenched with this hillbilly.

"Mr. Lunceford, I'm afraid it's a bit late today. If you still want to go out this evening after supper, I'd be happy to take you."

"No, no, I'll be checking out before noon. I'm not really a

fisherman, as I told you. I just thought as long as I was this far north . . ."

Jerry wiped his hands with a rag and tossed it into his tool kit, "Mind if I ask what *did* bring you up here?" It was not the kind of question a seasoned lodge owner did ask, and Jerry regretted it immediately. "Not that it's any of my business."

"Business," Mr. Lunceford replied. "Business, business, and more business."

"Not much business up here, except the timber business."

"I'm afraid there is more business in these mountains than timber." He paused and looked out at the lake. Three canvasback ducks paddled around the dock panhandling for yesterday's bread.

"There's more business in these mountains than you want to know."

Jerry remembered his wife's late night call to her mother in Pennsylvania: *He's taken the bait, isn't that a scream.* And Laszlo Batki in cabin 8 with his little flashlight, sifting other people's coffee grounds.

All his life he had hunted these hills and fished these lakes. He knew them as well as anyone. He had been a guide when he was still in high school.

"I don't exactly know what you're getting at, Mr. Lunceford. And, if it's a government secret, then I don't think I want to know anyway. But let me put it to you this way: Are you suggesting that I change the name Lake Umbagog Lodge & Cabins to Ground Zero Motel?" He smiled at this instance of his own wit.

And Lunceford appreciated his little joke out there in the wilderness. He felt like he was talking to a peer and colleague.

"I like Lake Umbagog Lodge & Cabins better," and then he added with charm, "for the meantime. Please thank Mrs. Kuncio for me. You've both been extremely kind. Next time I'll remember to bring my fishing gear."

AT THE RITZ

Her bottom half had fallen off. She didn't seem to notice and no one wanted to tell her. She was speaking of "men who had lost their lives to tigers." When she had lived in the Sunderbans she had dated many of them.

"In the long run," she sighed, "there is nothing more beautiful than a swimming tiger. So I guess you can say it was worth it." Long pause. "Poor boys. Poor dear, dear boys."

"Tigers are a serious problem in the Sunderbans," I said, sympathetically.

"435 deaths in 21 years," she said, "and that is only the official record and does not include unreported deaths."

I ordered another round of Mimosas.

"It's risky work with bees as well," I added, though I could feel the danger of heaping another horror on the pyre. "I mean, principally, nomad bees." Then, determined to strike an uplifting note, I added, "I as much as the next person relish their honey."

The upper torso of Valerie seemed to appreciate my effort.

"Recently they have begun to wear masks in the mangroves of the Sunderbans. Tigers apparently are mostly angered by the faces of men."

I sat there pondering this fascinating new thought and sipping my new drink.

AT THE RITZ

"One man took off his mask to enjoy his lunch and was immediately attacked. So there you go."

"Yes," I replied, rather meekly. I desperately needed to get her off this jag of dismemberment, this meditation on violent loss.

I should add here that Valerie is more attractive than a smoke tree, she has the beauty of the revenant, a sepulchral poise, and, at least to me, a deracinating effect that I, by the last vestiges of the most radiant gist, to borrow a phrase, of my most inner soul, to pass on a cliché, could not resist. And, of course, her eyes did resemble those of the sexier, large feline mammals so rare these days in Boston. And her hair was like a storm one had waited for all of one's life. Please, disappear me.

"People shouldn't be something they're not," she said, and stared into the mirror behind the bar. "I still don't know who I am. I was brought up to be a lady."

She was two halves of a lady, and a great lady at that. "You are a great lady," I reassured her, "It's just that you have paid dearly. It is an irony to me that Life seems so much more grueling since the discovery of penicillin."

"When I lived in Nubia, I had a pet cricket named Owen. He was such a comfort to me, and I miss him to this day. He was still living when I was forced to flee. He always slept on a petal of a cowslip. We had a fresh one flown in weekly. I only hope he died peacefully. I simply couldn't bear it if some ghastly sergeant stomped on him out of boredom or irritation from an imagined insult from some starving servant."

I didn't want to look into the mirror directly—I don't approve of narcissism, the sexual desire for one's own body; loathsome people, narcissists, in general—but from a more pathetic realm, I had a frail bit of curiosity to peek and see how we were holding up. I hadn't seen Valerie in ages. We were old chums, once lovers. From great distances I gleaned what I could from the tittle-tattle. I won't repeat it here, the marriages, divorces, fortunes won, fortunes lost, snakebite, air crash, ice cream factory in the jungles of hell. She's simply the dearest person I know, and I would readily behead anyone who spoke ill of her for one minute. But, now, I'm afraid I have stolen my sidelong glance into the mirror, and we both look terribly old and even strangely disheveled. But then, a moment later, I glanced again, and Valerie's bottom half had gotten up, on its own, it seemed, and attached itself seamlessly, and she looked like a young debutante of, say, eighteen years, much as when she first ravished me in the Gulf of Suez lo those many decades ago when I was recuperating from my bout with malaria.

"To the lady's room for me," she said, and walked off as if nothing had happened, as if nothing had ever happened.

"435 deaths in 21 years," she had said, "and that is only the official record and does not include unreported deaths."

I ordered another round of Mimosas and tried to imagine a few of the unreported deaths. No, I tried to imagine, to call into being, a swimming tiger, right there in the bar at the Ritz. And Owen on his cowslip petal.

When Valerie returned she kissed me on the cheek.

I could see that her bottom half was not really hers but someone else's. Or if not someone else's, then it was just a thing, something pieced together from odd bits of bamboo and straw and rubber plants, I don't know. Perhaps we had had too much to drink. I suppose these new thoughts ruled out the possibility of renting a room and making love with good, old Val.

"So how is it for you, Charlie? The library has been good to you? And Julie?"

"Julie's gone back to law school for the third time. I don't think she's suited for it, but nonetheless, that's what she's doing. And the board of directors hired a new head librarian who thinks I'm some kind of marginal eccentric who's mainly obsessed with the esoteric, and therefore put limits on my freedom."

"The Soul in a jar."

"Yes, that is it."

"What are we to do?"

It was almost dusk outside. Either I called home and lied about working late, or I gave myself over to Valerie for a few more hours, which, by now, clearly was the deepest lie bifurcated by the deepest truth I could hope to achieve in this life. For the next few minutes I was stalled in that ultimate, luxurious resting zone where everything was true and nothing was true. It's a terribly seductive island, very remote, and populated exclusively by transient beings, dancing, feasting, copulating, but only briefly, and then disappearing, to reappear, most likely, behind some counter of a cheap jewelry shop in a suburban mall, where one is permitted to live on forever.

THE INVISIBLE TWINS

Before he met Mary, Dan Jacobson's greatest achievements in life were in the areas of alcohol consumption and the seduction of young coeds. He was a genial, if slothful, man in his late thirties, who had never married or owned a car or a credit card. He just hadn't gotten around to these conventions of our culture. And some of this is what made him attractive to these coeds at the Junior College, I suppose. Dan had a lot of male friends, too, drinking buddies. Even in these health-conscious times, a hard-drinking crew. We didn't really trust non-drinkers; it was just a prejudice instilled into us by our love of recklessness, bravado, laughter and low tragedy. It's hard to say.

But then Dan met Mary and everything changed, at least with him. "What can I fix you?" I asked as usual.

"Perrier," he said.

"What do you mean, Perrier? I don't stock Perrier, pal. This isn't a sushi bar."

"Mary's convinced me to give up the booze. She's incredible, man. I'm in love, and I tell you I feel a lot better, too. I've been working-out, lifting weights and doing aerobics, I feel great."

It's a phase, I thought to myself. Dan always was impressionable. When he was going with that model, Jennifer, he had started wearing these thirty-dollar silk ties and his buddies had a few laughs behind his back. Now this.

"She's very successful, you know. She's pulling down eighty big ones a year."

"What the hell does she do?"

"She's a Herbalife saleswoman. She travels all over the country and gives those lectures on Herbalife and sells the product to prospective new salespeople. Eighty thousand a year, can you believe it?

"Frankly, pal, I haven't a clue what Herbalife *is*. But I'm sure it's not good for you. Probably kills all the important bacteria in our systems and replaces them with radioactive moss. I don't like the sound of it at all, and she isn't selling any of that stuff to me."

Dan did chuckle, for old time's sake, but I could tell my derision tweaked his new-found loyalty a bit. It was meant to.

"Well, John, say what you like, this is it for me. I'm in love for real this time and we're getting married."

I nearly fell over. "But you just met her. Why the hurry, slow down, pal."

"We want to have a baby, do it right, you know what I mean?"

"Marriage? A baby? You're going too fast for me. How long have you known her?"

"Two weeks, but I feel like I've known her my whole life. Everything else has been a warm-up for this one. We've already set the date, a month from now. We picked out a house yesterday. You wait till you see this sucker. It's a Victorian mansion, a quarter-million."

I couldn't believe what I was hearing, Dan Jacobson, master of the manse, a teetotaler, father.

I didn't see Dan again, nor did I meet his famous Mary, until the wedding. It was an opulent affair in a fancy Episcopalian church. The bride and groom arrived in a white, stretch limousine. The vows had been written by the happy couple, a practice, I admit, I hold in low esteem. I don't remember them now, but you know: "I promise to never raise my voice and to do the dishes every other night." Everybody there was dressed to the teeth, and I didn't recognize ninety percent of them anyway. Perhaps they had rented the congregation, a nice-looking bunch of stiffs if you ask me.

The reception was the really expensive part. The catering alone must have cost ten thousand. I began to notice these things, I began to add them up in my head. I had nothing better to do because I barely knew anyone and, as it turned out, there was a good reason. They were all into this Herbalife, the miracle substance about which I still knew nothing. I expressly changed the subject whenever it was mentioned, and of course it was mentioned constantly. This whole crowd, maybe two hundred people, had all gotten rich off of it. And I watched Dan mingling with them. It was hard to take.

After an hour or so of standing around by myself at the edge of an Olympic-sized swimming pool, Dan finally spotted me and brought Mary over for the introduction. He had said she was beautiful, and I suppose she was, but not to me. She had that dressed-for-success kind of smile that made me wonder if her teeth were sharp as razors. Her steel-blue eyes assessed my situation and dismissed me as not in her league, no Herbalife possibilities as either buyer or seller.

"We're going to have the baby next May," she said. "Dan can

take paternity-leave, he's already checked that out. I can travel up to the eighth month, and I'll stay home for six weeks after the birth. Got to get back out there on the road, there's such a demand."

"Sounds good," I said. "I'm really happy for both of you." Both Dan and Mary were drinking non-alcoholic champagne. I sipped a Coke to help celebrate this amazing union, but soon took French leave.

Most of the old gang—Sal, Rick, Willy and Patrice—said they were happy for Dan, that he looked good, that he was really in love, that he had even gotten a hell of a good deal—but there had to be some suspicion, too. I mean the way it happened, overnight. Suddenly Dan's in this mansion, suddenly Dan who we had seen put away enough vodka over the years to float a battleship, as they say. And also the baby. Yeah, Dan had a sentimental side, this was well known, but that Mary didn't look too maternal to me. Her career came first, this was clear. She knew it could fall through any time, one year, two years, who can say how long these fads will last? And no retirement plan. Just grab what you can now while the dummy product is hot. She had already made a bundle, there was no denying that. And now Dan was living very well, thanks to her. I wouldn't have wanted to be in his shoes.

I was having a few beers over at Sal's apartment about a month later when he hit me with some of the talk that was going around. "I've got at least three sources that say she's into S&M. She was an alkie, too, you know, for years before she found the road to success. Strange woman. Do you think Dan can handle it?"

"I don't know nothing these days. Something doesn't strike me as right, but maybe we're all just jealous. Maybe they're as madly in love as they say. She's pushing forty-two, you know. She hasn't got that much time, and her eggs are awfully well traveled, that's all I'll say. I wish them luck."

Sal was having a pretty rough time of it himself these days, out of work, recently separated from Josie. "It just all seems too good to be true," he said, stubbing out another Lucky.

"Yeah," I concurred, "Dan did tell me they were humping like bunnies to try and conceive right away to coincide with his paternity-leave, or whatever it's called. Can you imagine that, the man taking off 'cause the woman had a kid?"

"I guess you and I are living in the dark ages still, hey John?"

It's not as though I was completely caught up in Dan and Mary's every move. Weeks, even months, passed without my giving more than a passing thought to their situation. But I was curious about this business of Mary's biological time clock, as they say. Who is "they"? I don't know, it's just a phrase I don't remember hearing much until recently. Now I hear it all the time. Everybody's clock is running out, an exhausted species. And also Mary had said to me at the wedding reception—it comes back to me now—she said to me that she wanted to have a baby to prove to her friends—presumably the hordes of Herbalife gentry—"that she could do it all." And this had stuck in my craw.

When a year had passed without a single invitation to their new home, I pretty much let go of Dan in my mind. Mary was calling the shots, and Dan jumped when she said jump. I knew from Patrice—our Nigerian Marxist philosopher friend—that Mary was not pregnant, that Dan had postponed his paternity leave, and that Mary had traveled to over seventy-five cities to deliver her pitch since they were married. Beyond that, he didn't know much, except that they were still trying to get Mary pregnant at every possible pit-stop. And Dan was in charge of overseeing all the elaborate renovations of the mansion while Mary traveled. Given what I knew of Dan's lack of domestic experience and his hitherto faulty sense of responsibility, my imagination strained to complete this picture.

And then late one night Dan called. I didn't feel that warmly at first, but when he announced that Mary was finally pregnant I let down my protective shield and tried to match the jubilation in his voice. "Congratulations, Danny-boy, you'll make a great father." There was a moment of silence, then a kind of sardonic laugh. "Thanks, John." It seemed we didn't have that much to talk about—the house, Mary's travels, the baby. Dan asked about my work, but I didn't feel like dwelling on it, what with the importance of his own news. So, rather clumsily, we apologized for not being in touch, promised to change all that now.

I ran into Dan's mother at the supermarket some time after the call. I congratulated her, I don't know what for, for bringing Dan into the world, I guess, for playing her part in this birth-chain. Dan was an only child, and of course she was pleased and proud, but seemed to dwell more on Mary's success and the impressive cost of their new house, the changes and lack of change in her son. She had seen them only twice since the wedding and seemed pained by this, but would have never admitted this. Dan had sponged off his parents well into his thirties, and this sudden flaunting of riches must have stirred mixed feelings. Nonetheless, all bitternesses aside, she was to be a grandmother at long last, she had nearly given up on Dan ever settling down. There had been some sweet and attractive prospects along the way, but Dan had always let them go, had always insisted on his right to have some "sidekickers," as he called them, to complement his current "main squeeze." But now, Mrs. Jacobson fully believed his claim of complete loyalty to Mary and all that she stood for. At this point I couldn't help myself and asked, "And what does she stand for?"

Mrs. Jacobson took the question, which could easily enough have been interpreted as rude, in stride, having, apparently, already asked herself that question. "Oh, I don't know. I think Mary believes in success, hard work rewarded by material gain." I agreed with that, I couldn't have agreed more, but Dan's mother spoke the words with a careful smile, as though this indeed summarized the best of the American work ethic, and wasn't that what all good families were built on?

But, for me, a mild sense of loss persisted. I didn't really care about Dan anymore and, while I never confessed this to any of the guys, I sensed some distancing on their parts as well. His name came up only if someone chanced upon him in town doing errands. The reports got thinner and thinner. Willy, Dan's old baseball buddy, told us that Mary was going to have twins. None of us betrayed much interest, except to say that she had probably been taking fertility drugs since they had had so much trouble conceiving. Dan, father of twins!

THE INVISIBLE TWINS

My own life drifted or bounced along without major incident until one spring day I paused to assess my situation and found, without any great surprise, that I had dug myself into a rut that was beginning to stifle and suffocate. I was married young and stayed married through my twenties; divorced and stayed divorced through my thirties. Maybe my clock was running out, I chuckled to myself. I talked to Sal about this several times. Finally, he too decided to "liquidate," sell what assets we had, and make a last stab at the Grand Tour. I quit my job at the magazine, successfully advertised and sold my old Peugeot in one of the local papers. My boss at the magazine told me I might have my job back if I didn't stay away too long. She didn't say how long was too long.

Sal and I lasted a little over two months in Amsterdam. It was one continual party, and we seemed to be handed about from one group to another, never paying rent, sleeping with more women than I had known in all of the past decade, with no strings, no promises, just the convenience of ready flesh and desire. We acted like a couple of twenty-year-olds just out of the Navy. Occasionally, we even paid prostitutes just to do our part in stimulating the economy of our tiny host nation. We sat up all night with bands of squatters smoking hashish and drinking strong beer and coffee.

Something had definitely been reawakened in both of us. Sal was already talking of permanently settling there, though work permits were a problem. Our new friends promised to help. Hugo and Jan, both journalists, knew people who could help.

Just being on the continent and meeting so many new types of people had already had a tonic effect on me, and I longed to see more. I already sensed that there were possibilities I had never before even considered.

"I want to head south, to Spain, maybe Morocco, Sal. You coming or staying?"

But Sal had found himself a girl and something seemed to be developing between them. He was staying home with her more in her apartment the past few weeks, and it was good for him. I hadn't seen him as happy in years.

We made our goodbyes at the train station and, though I couldn't have known it then, I would never see Sal again.

I spent the next sixteen months in a small fishing village in Southern Spain, letting a lifetime of tensions pour out from the bottoms of my feet onto the Mediterranean sands and, in general, reflecting on how good life could be. The food, the people, the sun, all healing. The gypsy woman who lived in the ruins next to my modest house had thirteen children and no plumbing or electricity, and yet she sang from morning until night and loved those half-naked, crazy, filthy kids. One of the middle-class Spanish ladies I had gotten to know asked her one day if the children weren't a terrible burden, if they weren't just too much for her to feed and keep out of trouble; and the toothless old hag (she was actually only 36 but appeared a well-worn 72) replied with a cackle that God loved her because He had given her so many children who would look after her in her old age.

Each day I drank the local wines with fishermen and affable smugglers or shopkeepers. I wrote each day in a journal and read my secondhand paperbacks left behind by previous English-speaking travelers. Very few people back in the States knew where I was, and that was fine with me. I thought less and less about what I had left behind, just as I thought little of the future. If the sun was out, that was enough. What new flower bloomed in the garden colored my day, along with Angelica's singing.

I could have let go, cut the string to the kite of my life, and never returned to the scene of my former life. But after a year and a half, I knew I was drifting away to become something unrecognizable and, ultimately—hateful word!—unuseful. Enough had changed, enough had been shed, and I couldn't help but hope this time had been more than an escape, it had also signaled a new beginning.

Maisie, my former boss, was my boss again. She and my other former colleagues remarked on the changes in me. And, though I was loathe to admit it, I welcomed the structure of working back into my life. It wasn't long before I was stopping by for drinks at the old haunts. Old friends looked new, even those who hadn't changed that much.

"So how old would Dan's twins be by now?" I asked Willy.

"I guess they'd be . . ." he paused, "you know I haven't seen Dan once since before you ever left the country. So how would I know? He's dropped all his old friends, as far as I know." I detected more than a note of bitterness. Willy and Dan had been the closest friends in the group. I found myself really wanting to know how Dan was, what had become of his life. I imagined him thriving in the mansion with full-time nannies looking after the twins. But this kind of imagining was no longer built on anything.

THE INVISIBLE TWINS

One morning, a few days later, I called Mrs. Jacobson on the phone. At one time I had thought she liked me, thought I was a positive influence on her slothful son, but at first it seemed as though she barely remembered me.

"I was living in Europe for a while," I explained, "and I was just wondering how Dan and Mary were doing, I hadn't heard anything . . ."

"Oh, I suppose they're doing very well. They have bought a hideaway somewhere in the Caribbean, I can never remember the name of the island."

"And the twins, what did Mary have? How are they?"

"I've never seen them myself," she said, and I knew I had struck a sore spot.

"Never seen them? How could that be?"

"Well," she said, "They sent me one picture, but I don't believe it. Neither Dan nor Mary are in the picture to prove it's their twins, and I just don't believe they ever had anything but money, twins of money."

WELCOME SIGNS

Ever since her return home from the hospital, Mrs. Norris found herself taking extreme delight in the observation of birds and other little creatures that visited her yard. The goldfinch that perched on her bed of daisies each morning and early evening nabbing small insects brightened her spirits and helped her to forget her still-nagging pain. And the day a scarlet tanager flittered from tree to tree in plain view of her kitchen window Mrs. Norris felt no pain at all. It was heaven-sent, as bright and shining as hope itself.

She called to her only daughter, Susie, to come quick.

"He's come to visit us all the way from Peru. Look, Susie, he's our first scarlet tanager. Have you ever seen anything redder than that?"

Susie had pouted in her room the whole time Mrs. Norris was hospitalized, and was now sensitive to any change she sensed in her mother.

"He changes color in the autumn. He doesn't want to be seen in the winter wearing that bright red coat of feathers. Isn't he smart?"

Susie pulled away from her mother's arms and clutched her doll.

When Mr. Norris came home from work at five, Mrs. Norris

told him about the visitation of the tanager. Mr. Norris did not know what a tanager was, but was happy she had had a good day.

"What's for dinner?" he asked, as always, pleased that a semblance of the old routine was returning.

"Fish and corn-on-the-cob. Did you have a good day? Did Garrett get his report in on time?"

"Oh, you know Garrett. It was on time, but I think he made up some of the figures. His mind's on baseball this time of year. The rest is just going through the motions. Lydia does a pretty good job of covering for him." Mr. Norris picked up the newspaper and scanned the front page. "They say it's going to rain tomorrow."

"I saw the skunk again last night, Clifford, after you went to bed. He's not afraid of me. I was standing five feet from him for the longest time. I followed him around the yard with the flashlight. I think he would have let me pet him, really. He's beautiful."

"You better watch yourself. You get yourself sprayed and you'll be sleeping in the tent for the rest of the summer."

Susie, who was playing in her room, thought it strange that her mother should follow a skunk around the yard late at night. She hoped nobody else would find out. She was certain nobody else's mother had ever done such a disgusting thing. A skunk, p.u.

"By the way," Mr. Norris said, "I've invited the Cummings over for dinner on Saturday. Are you up to it? They've been asking about you and I thought it might be good for you. Okay?"

"I'm sure I'll manage." But, in truth, Mrs. Norris wished her family wasn't in such a hurry to get back to normal. She liked living in the twilight world with furry and feathery friends. The family of wrens in the birdhouse on the front-porch was more riveting to her now than all the dinner-guests she had ever cooked for in the past. Their little ones were about to fly from the nest any day now and she didn't want to miss the event. She had witnessed many families raise their chicks in that house, but this year it was especially important to her that all go well. After dinner Susie asked permission to go across the street to play with her friend Tamika. Mrs. Norris cleaned the dishes while Mr. Norris puttered with a table he was making in the basement.

She saw something moving on the edge of the woods that abuts their property. It was something large and unfamiliar and she called to Mr. Norris in the basement. "Come here, Cliff. There's an ostrich out here. Come see!"

"What the hell are you yelling about? I can't hear you." She was always yelling at him when he was working in the basement. It was one thing that had annoyed him for years, and that hadn't changed.

"An ostrich, there's an ostrich in the woods."

"Are you out of your mind, woman?" Reluctantly he put down his tools and climbed the steps to the kitchen. "Now what is it?"

"Here, look." She handed him the binoculars that she seemed to carry everywhere since she had gotten back.

"By God, it's a wild turkey. Well isn't that something. That's the first time I've seen one of those since we've lived here."

The huge bird could have been mistaken for a small ostrich, he had to grant her that. And now that he thought about it, it was pretty funny. "An ostrich," he chuckled. "You'll be seeing elephants soon." And then he returned to the basement.

The sun was setting as Mrs. Norris finished the dishes and polished the counter. It was going to be a beautiful sunset, the air had a slight chill to it, her favorite weather.

"Do you want to go for a walk?" she shouted down the stairs at Mr. Norris.

"What? What is it you want now?"

"I said, do you want to go for a walk? Just a short one while Susie is at the Smiths?"

"I want to finish the table tonight. You go on, maybe I'll catch up with you."

The sky in the west was pink and lavender and shot through with drifting tangerine islands. Mrs. Norris walked the road with a sense of purpose, knowing the best vantage-point from which to view the final sinking of the sun. It was a meadow, just twenty minutes by foot from her home. A single, dappled grey horse grazed there through all the seasons of the year, and today she positioned herself so that the sun would set directly in back of the horse. She had no name for the beast, but she was fond of him, especially now. He stared at her and whisked his tail back and forth, scattering flies.

When there was nothing left but a faint orange glow on the horizon, Mrs. Norris turned and continued her walk in the other direction. She was sorry Mr. Norris had not joined her. They had walked together in the evenings for many years, but then he began to find excuses. And Susie was afraid of the dark.

A slight breeze rippled the silvery birch leaves. The grim and tedious weeks in the hospital drifted through her mind like a half-forgotten dream. She would breathe this air, here, now, and be grateful to be alive. She winked at the little bunny watching her from crazy old Mrs. Parks' vegetable garden.

Mrs. Parks' two goats leaned their heads over their wooden fence and neighed greeting to her as she passed. She stopped to pat their heads and scratch their noses. "What a funny world we live in," she said to them, half-expecting some form of agreement from them, and then getting it. When she returned from her walk, Mr. Norris was propped up in bed reading a mystery novel. "I wish you would have come," she said to him, situating herself on the edge of the bed beside him. "The sunset was gorgeous, and I had the funniest thing happen."

"Yes," he said, lowering his reading glasses.

"It was just down at the corner. I was walking along and I spotted a little field mouse by the side of the road. The moon was very bright or I wouldn't have seen him at all."

"A mouse, yes. You spotted a mouse."

"Yes, and it was munching on something. I could see that. And it was sitting up munching on something."

"Yes. Quite fascinating. Go on."

"Well, you see, it looked right at me and didn't seem to be afraid one bit."

"Yes."

"And, well, I decided to try to get closer to him."

"You wanted to get close to this mouse, have I got this right?"

"And so I got down on my hands and knees and started crawling toward him."

"This is quite a story, if you don't mind my saying so. Most women are terrified of mice, and my wife is crawling toward one on her hands and knees in the gravel."

"And, Clifford, you wouldn't believe it. I put my face within inches of his and he wasn't in the least nervous. He just kept munching on what turned-out to be a dried worm, very sandy, I would think. And I crouched like that for fifteen minutes, just watching him. He was the cutest thing I've ever seen in my life. His tiny little paws washing his face between bites, and his tiny pointed nose, his whiskers and eyes and ears. Really, I was completely enchanted by this little fellow."

"Well, I'm speechless, Winnie. That's quite a story. Meanwhile, Susie was wondering where you were. I put her to bed, but she's upset about something. Tamika hit her or something. Anyway, it appears they had some kind of fight or other. You had better go say goodnight to her."

Mrs. Norris agreed.

The next afternoon Mr. Norris called Bill Cummings from the office to cancel the dinner they had planned on Saturday.

"I don't think Winnie is up to it yet," he explained. "She's still a bit fragile."

DESPAIR ICE CREAM

The Annual Arts and Crafts Fair was set up in the town park, six or seven large tents busy with potters and painters and musicians and story-tellers and everything you could ever want. People came from all around in campers and vans plastered with bizarre bumper stickers. It was really some kind of collection of humanity that is better left undescribed, backwoods mall-people with unhygienic habits, people with barely lawful fetishes, aggressive hats, and overweight children. Still, arts and crafts can be elevating.

One such overweight boy, about fifteen years of age, stood beside his short, plump mother reading the buttons a left-over hippie was trying to sell. Even the funnier buttons seemed to make them sad, or sadder. The boy pointed to one that read EAT McSHIT & DIE. The mother slapped his hand and they strolled off toward one of the many food concessions. They each ordered a huge bratwurst with sauerkraut. An old man stood beside them doing tricks with a day-glo yo-yo, rock-the-baby and walk-the-dog. He seemed immensely pleased with himself, and it seemed to anyone watching that the man had almost certainly devoted the better part of his life to mastering these tricks.

"Lenny," the mother said to her son, "Go get us some more napkins." The boy's shirt-tails were out and the front of his shirt sported at least a dozen large grease and juice stains.

When Lenny returned with the napkins he couldn't find his

mother at first. There were life-sized puppets punching one another in the nose and he watched them for a while, not really concerned. He would find her, she would find him, they always did. He accompanied her everywhere, to movies, lectures, shopping. She couldn't seem to do anything by herself, or he felt sorry for her, or she felt sorry for him. He couldn't sort it all out, and vaguely resented that he should even have to. After all, he was only fifteen.

"Here." She had come up behind him and held out a massive cone of cotton candy. She had one for herself as well, already half-eaten. They ate in silence and Lenny's face once again was discolored with blotches of pink spun sugar. Loudspeakers announced a glassblowing demonstration in tent #6 and mother and son exchanged knowing stares. They had seen the glass blowing demonstration eight years running and this time they were not going to fall for it. There really was nothing new from year to year, and yet their decision to attend each year was not even voluntary at this point. Just as it was not a decision to head for the ice-cream stand once they had finished the cotton candy, double dips of vanilla for both of them.

Something about this particular day had Lenny on the verge of tears, but he held them back and bit his lip. "Why," he wanted to say, "Why won't you tell me anything? For God's sake, it's my life, too." But he knew too well that all questions regarding his birth and his father were forbidden. She hurt, too. Yes, she hurt, too. And so they finished their ice creams, and ambled into a tent where a college student was telling a story about two baby calves lost on a mountaintop. Lenny held onto his mother's arm and squeezed it several times. She patted his hair into place.

RUNNING FOR YOUR LIFE

Three little plastic pigs had crawled into my shoes in the middle of the night. We still had a river to ford in the morning. The rains were coming down. And a man by the name of Bad Bud Rosenblatt was breathing down our necks with an electric can-opener. A middle-level lieutenant from the phone company had put a price on our heads: $3.00. And Bad Bud Rosenblatt was flat broke.

Tina turned in her sleep to ask if, once we got to Philadelphia, we could take the horses onto the subway.

"I suppose," I said, "if they'll fit. But, you know, Tina, I'm not sure if they have an underground in Philly. Or, if they once had one, if it's still there."

An hour later the rain had stopped. The horses were practicing their flamenco on a rock nearby. A family of bobcats stepped gingerly over our heads.

"If there are subways," I said, "I hope they have maps in them, because I don't think I'll recognize anything. Father said we lived there for three or four years, but I think that was before we were born."

"Do you remember the day Buddy Rosenblatt crashed his bicycle into the milk truck?"

"No," I said. "But didn't you wrap his head in your shirt or something?"

"They said I did. I have a good memory for all sorts of blood, and don't remember any of his."

"They say he's a bloodless killer."

"What does that mean?"

"They talk too much."

"'They' also say Father loved Aunt Isabel all those years he worked at the Dairy Queen."

"My God, Tina, is nothing sacred to you anymore?"

"Sure, brother. I've got a long list of Still Sacred, though, actually, I've just recently begun to refer to that particular list as More Sacred. You want a peek? In no particular order, I can just make out through the Stygian smoke and mist—a long, hot bath, a tall tumbler of bourbon, some slow lovin', a few Billie Holiday songs . . . You want more?"

"You're a piece of work, you know that? I remember the Thanksgiving you smashed Aunt Sophie's tiara with your drumstick. She wouldn't stop crying the rest of the afternoon."

"Who the hell did she think she was anyway, the Queen of Rumania?"

"Mother had to hide behind the lilac bush in the backyard until she could stop laughing."

"Mother was a good egg."

"She was the best."

The rain had stopped. From time to time I glimpsed several pairs of eyes carving us up into tasty bites from the edge of the clearing. But there was no blood, all things considered. A quarter-moon was gaining strength, or at least clarity. The actual strength wobbled, vacillated, doubted its own strength.

Tina's silhouette was striped. The horses were necking quietly in a stand of birch trees. "He never actually beat her," I said.

"Mother might have welcomed a good spanking," Tina said, taking a deep drag from her last cigarillo, "what with her circulation problems and all."

"It was you who could do no wrong. Mother, with all the love in the world, only reminded him of his failure. All of her kisses he twisted into remonstrances. And I was the insurance policy that guaranteed his failure would live on, would not be forgotten, his name forever in ignominy."

"That's not true, brother. Father knew how hard you tried. When you were on the track team he never missed a meet."

"And I never won a race, not once did I win."

"But you ran harder than all the rest; everyone could see that, you were that beautiful and we were so proud of you."

"I always thought I was going to burst into flame."

"That's funny. You never told me that, but one of my clearest memories from those years is praying in the bleachers that you wouldn't burst into flames. Even seated so far away from you I could feel the fire coming out of you. Father could feel it too. He never said as much, but I always knew he could feel it."

It was almost light now. Birds were shaking their heads and ungluing their eyes. Bad Bud Rosenblatt was snoring on a little pallet he had made himself sometime during the night. "Shouldn't we cover him with something?" I asked.

"Buddy's such a wimp," Tina said. "Always catching a cold when he should be catching his quarry."

I grabbed Tina by her shoulders and forced her to look me in the eyes. I could see the years, neatly labeled and stacked in boxes. The stuff that wouldn't fit was burned long ago in an abandoned field no one would ever visit again. Or if some lost kid stumbled upon it he wouldn't know what it was. He'd just kick it a few times and walk on, his poor mother pulling her hair and calling his name from a porch in the clouds.

But I could also see the mountains in back of me reflected in Tina's eyes, the mountains we would try to cross today.

She gave me a good bearcub slap across the face and started to laugh. "Let's just see if we can manage to get back up on the horses."

I kissed her hard on the mouth. "Let's leave them here," I said. "This is like home to them." Our chances weren't that good.

"If ever there was a time to be afraid ... but I'm not. I remember when Buddy's sister died. Mother said. 'Well, at least she got to taste chocolate cake.' I thought about that for years."

"I remember father crying at the funeral; it was as if she were his only child. He couldn't talk to us for days. Do you think he'll remember us?"

I couldn't answer. I was suddenly anxious to get started. I felt as if I barely knew Tina. Tina the ballerina long ago disappeared, Tina the lepidopterist and Tina the tea-leaf reader had fallen overboard during a storm early on in the passage, shortly after her brother the runner had burst into flames, not during a team track meet but during a private session. In each case there were no witnesses, and not even any questions afterwards. That is what always seemed so strange to me: that not only must one disappear on one's own.... I couldn't complete the thought, I didn't want to.

"It won't matter," I said.

Bad Bud Rosenblatt was beginning to stretch and make waking sounds, the bounty hunter, the dreaming witness. Without speaking a word we placed a handful of wooden matches and a large chunk of brown bread beside Bud and made haste for the mule trail that would take us out of this fake paradise and back to the homeless world where we belonged.

ROBES

She must have been the tallest nun in the world and, standing there at the streetlight, a crowd was beginning to gather about her. Punks and flower vendors and dirty-faced little girls stared up at her in wonder. At first she tried to ignore them and gazed straight ahead at the red light, but the crude little bumpkins had never seen a nun before, and certainly not one of such towering grandeur. She radiated an inner peace even as she was scrutinized.

"My name is Sister Theodosa, and I suppose you are wondering just how tall I am."

None of the urchins dared to speak, so powerful was her presence. They scuffled around one another for a better view. Some of them backed up a few steps to get a better advantage.

"Well, it is my secret," she whispered.

Ollie Cunningham, one of the worst troublemakers in his fourth grade class, had an overwhelming urge to touch her black robes, and he did it. She touched the top of his head and he thought he was going to explode, right there. Becky Maddox burst out laughing. She was in his class and was the best speller in the fourth grade. She even knew how to spell the capital of Swaziland, and what kind of useless information is that?

Ollie now stared at the hand which extended from the huge

folds of Sister Theodosa's black sleeve. Sister Theodosa knew too well what it was to be a curiosity, she knew how it had shaped her life, and now she loved God and his little children.

"Come here," she said to Ollie. Wade and Leon were giggling uncontrollably, but Ollie didn't care. He had never been in love before, not like this.

"I bet your name is Ollie, am I right?" And Ollie nearly fainted. "Don't be frightened, I'm not a witch. I know your mother, Edith Cunningham, formerly Edith Butler. We were in school together, she has sent me pictures of you." But still Ollie's heart was racing, some magic had entered his life and he could not take his eyes off of Sister Theodosa. It was a struggle for him to speak, but he knew he must.

"My mother . . ." he said, but could not go on.

"That's all right, Ollie. Would you do me a favor?" Ollie shook his head yes, he would do anything for her. "Would you take me to your home?" He shook his head yes again and looked around at the others, feeling both proud and terrified. How could he walk beside one so tall and dressed so strangely?

"Come now. I've traveled a great distance. Let me hold your hand and let's be on our way."

Ollie blushed but complied with her wish. He expected Leon or Wade to call out "sissy," but instead they followed the giant lady in black from a safe distance. She looked as if she should be the object of worship, a whole religion might spring up around her feet. She was so calm and graceful she might go waltzing with the Pope of a spring evening. Wade looked at Leon as if he were crazy for having such thoughts. It's not that this lady demanded respect, she simply, and obviously, deserved it. Perhaps she would move to their town and everything would be different.

"I never knew your father," Sister Theodosa was saying to Ollie.

"He wasn't around much anyway," Ollie replied. "I've got some letters from him in a box, and a picture. I guess he just liked to travel, that's what mom says, that he was a traveling man."

"I bet he loved you very much."

"Not so's you'd notice."

"Some people just don't know how to show it, but they love in their own way."

"I don't think he loved me, at least not much. He would have stayed home more."

Sister Theodosa tousled Ollie's hair, and Ollie didn't care what the kids behind him thought, he knew he was the lucky one.

When Edith Cunningham greeted Sister Theodosa at the door, Ollie was surprised to hear his mother address this strange and magical lady as "Vera."

She said, "Vera, you've come, how thoughtful. I see you recognized my little scoundrel from his pictures. I hope he wasn't rude to you." Ollie was pained by this suggestion.

"Quite the contrary, he's been a perfect gentleman."

Edith looked around Vera's robes at the little congregation of followers her old friend had attracted. A silent vigil had formed on the other side of the street.

"And what about those hooligans, did they give you any trouble?"

"None whatsoever, Edith. I must say, you appear well, in spite of your grief." She embraced Edith, a trifle uncertain of her role.

"I'm fine, really I am. I suppose it's terrible to admit it, but there is a certain amount of relief. I mean, I never knew when . . . Oh, how rude of me. Please come in, please make yourself comfortable. I'll just pick up and fix us something nice and cool."

Ollie stood by himself off to one side and looked around the room. He had never thought about it before, but suddenly it occurred to him: *We're poor. We're poor and I never even knew it.* He thought a person like Sister Theodosa, or Vera, whatever her name was, must live in a splendid palace with servants and thrones, while he and his mom watched their broken TV on that couch with the springs sticking through and the arms half worn away.

"Ollie, come help with the lemonade," his mother called from the kitchen. Vera, Sister Theodosa, had not seen her friend, Edith, in ten long years. That last summer they had shared a cabin on a remote beach. Each day they swam and sunbathed. They shopped at a nearby village. They picnicked. They read long novels and talked. Vera sensed an awakening in herself, a possibility for total love, but when she confronted these feelings in herself she was forced to conclude that Edith was innocent of the same ardor, that for her it was simply a summer free of the complication of young men's inconstancy.

"Vera, I wish you would tell Ollie how important it is that he do well in school. The boy is lucky he hasn't been forced to repeat this past year. He was sent to the principal three times. He doesn't know how rough it can be in the world without a proper education." Edith had brought in a tray with three glasses and a pitcher of lemonade and was clearing a place for the tray on the coffee table.

"What subjects do you like best, Ollie?"

Ollie saw how gently she deflected his mother's criticism.

"Geography, I guess I like geography, reading about foreign places."

"Do you want to travel when you're older?"

"I guess."

"Where would you like to go?"

As luck would have it, now he couldn't think of any place. He tried to remember all the pictures, pictures of natives in Africa, pictures of old cathedrals in other parts of the world, but he couldn't remember names.

"I'd like to go to Swaziland," he said, and then felt a cold shiver run through his stomach, it was such a stupid thing to say. But Vera sensed his embarrassment.

"You've got me on that one," she said. "Is it in Africa?"

"I think so. The King has six hundred children."

"Vera," Edith interrupted, "would you like to change clothes? I mean , no one will know. I just thought you might be more comfortable."

Vera didn't seem upset with Edith's suggestion. In fact, the idea refreshed and stimulated her. Ollie, on the other hand, could not imagine her in anything but the majestic black robes. He was afraid of losing her, her specialness, as though she would reappear in common dress and treat him exactly as his mother did—

as though he could do nothing right. "He had one hundred wives," he said.

"Yes," Vera said, "I'd like to change. Thank you for suggesting it, Edith. You can't imagine . . ." She didn't finish the thought, but took her bag into Edith's room and closed the door behind her.

"Ollie, I'm going to call Mr. Grady and tell him that you will be down to pick up a bottle of wine for me."

"But Mom . . ."

"You do as I say. Here's five dollars. Be sure to bring me the change. Now get going."

Only Leon still sat vigil on the curb. He was whittling on a stick, but stood up when he saw Ollie come down the front steps of the house.

"What's she like?" he asked. "Can she perform magic tricks?"

Ollie didn't feel like talking to Leon, but there wasn't much he could do to discourage him from walking with him to the store.

"Does she really know your mother? How can you talk to her?"

Ollie had always felt that his mother secretly blamed him for his father's staying away so much of the time. He didn't really know Vera, but already he wished she would stay on with them. Maybe then his mother would forgive him. *Forgive him*, he didn't know what he had done, aside from the little things, and being born. He assumed that was it: his father hadn't wanted to have a child, maybe they were too poor, and this meant that his mother couldn't travel with him.

"Yeah, they were friends before I was born, I guess."

"Does she always dress like that?"

"Leon, I don't know much myself. I just met her today. All I know is that she's real nice to me and that she has two names. My mother calls her Vera."

Leon was even more fascinated now, how anyone could have two different names mystified him, as if she could turn into a leopard if she wanted.

"Are you mad at me?" he asked Ollie.

"No, I've just got to hurry, that's all."

When he returned from the store, he found his mother and Vera sitting on the back porch. Vera had been transformed into a startling wonderwork of womanhood. She wore a pair of faded bluejeans and a white t-shirt that said I LOVE NEW YORK in red across the front. But what stole Ollie's attention most powerfully was the sight of her long, dark hair. It altered her face in ways he could not explain.

"Well, what do you think, Ollie? Which do you prefer, Sister Theodosa or plain, old Vera Sims?" She did not mean to put him on the spot, just to include him in their discussion.

"I like both of you," he said, and he meant it.

"Very diplomatic, your son is."

"It's you, I think he has a crush on you, Vera."

Ollie went back inside to avoid further embarrassment. He went to the refrigerator and got himself a Coke. He could hear the two women talking.

"...it's my last chance," Vera was saying, "If I don't leave now..."

ROBES

"You could stay with us for awhile until . . ."

"I still think of our summer . . ."

"I don't know, Vera, I've never . . . Ollie . . ."

"I could love Ollie. You know that, Edith. I could be the father he never had . . ."

DIANE AND MIRIAM

The two young women had developed some kind of friendship over the past three months while working together part-time at the Cozy Corner Nursing Home, though in fact they came from very different backgrounds. Diane lived in a comfortable section of town with her parents and three siblings, while Miriam lived in a poorer neighborhood with only her mother whom she called by her first name, Greta. Miriam told Diane right off that her father had been merely a one-night stand, but that, according to Greta, he had been tall and handsome. This was some consolation, Diane thought to herself. Miriam also told Diane in their very first conversation that Greta was crazy. Diane didn't know if she should take this seriously or not. People say funny things just for effect sometimes. Still, she didn't have friends like Miriam at her school: everyone pretended to be so proper and on some kind of upward-bound track. So she found Miriam's candor refreshing.

As the weeks went by Miriam continued to amaze Diane with other kinds of confessions. She told Diane that she went to a certain discotheque at least three nights a week. She would go late and stand alone in the long hallway leading into the club. Eventually some stranger would approach her and she would go home with him and have sex. Once she went home with a rich man when she was having her period and she stained his sheets and he made her wash them right after they finished. Diane was simultaneously enthralled and appalled. What kind of life was this anyway? What kind of person? Still, she listened and occasionally asked questions. Apparently nothing could shock Miriam, so she asked her if she ever asked for money and Miriam said, "No, never. Of course not."

Diane never told her family or other friends about Miriam. She was certain they couldn't understand, especially since she was not sure she did. But the fact remained: Miriam was her friend, she couldn't really figure her out or criticize her because that's just the way she was.

"Why don't you come over to my place after work tonight," Miriam asked Diane one night.

"And do what?" Diane asked in return, discovering a pocket of fear in herself. She hadn't meant to insult Miriam and Miriam didn't appear to take it as such.

"Just mess around. We'll think of something. Greta's going out. It's safe. The old hag has a date, can you believe it? At her age. I'd like to see the gentleman caller that would stoop to taking Greta out on a date. Ha!"

"Okay, but I can only stay a couple of hours." For the rest of the shift Diane tried to put it out of her mind, but in fact she was apprehensive and she didn't really know why. She liked Miriam.

She had rarely ever been in that part of town, and it was a bit scary in the dark. There were drunks asleep in alleys, and what she took to be pimps and hoodlums sizing everybody up as they drove by. The fear tinkling in the pit of her stomach was also excitement, excitement for the unknown and for the sense of danger and adventure that these sleazy, rough late-night street people aroused in her. Diane's parents would have died if they had known where their daughter was.

Miriam's apartment was another kind of shock: it was *so* dreary. Everything was faded pink and grey and dark green. The over-stuffed chair in the corner was hardly any color at all, and the couch sagged and looked like one one would see discarded at the dump. "That's where Greta sleeps," Miriam said pointing to the couch. "I've got the only bedroom. In here," she said, crossing the living room.

Miriam's room had a full-sized mattress on the floor and a pair of matching chairs with yellow plastic seats. But what caught Diane's eye first were the posters of nude or bikini-clad women on all the walls. She looked at each of them in turn with growing puzzlement.

"I'm not a dyke, if that's what you're thinking. My god, you of all people should know that, from what I've told you. I just like to see other women's bodies, to compare, you know, to see how I'm doing."

"Oh I never thought you were a dyke, give me a break. I've just never looked at naked pictures before. Of men or women. Maybe once my brother showed me a magazine, but I didn't really look. I thought it was, you know, forbidden."

"Well, there's no time like the present. I've got *stacks* of nudie magazines in my closet."

Miriam immediately produced one such stack and the two of them sat on Miriam's bed and proceeded to look through them, Diane's curiosity sparked sufficiently to join in commenting on every variation of breast size and curve.

DIANE AND MIRIAM

"I wish I had really dark nipples like that," Miriam said, "large and very dark. You've got nice long legs, by the way, I've been meaning to tell you that. Men like long legs. Mine should be about two inches longer to go with my torso, you know what I mean?"

"I think you have nice legs. Besides, looks aren't everything." Miriam looked at her as if she were insane.

"Better that the breasts aren't too big, because then men will only like you when you're young. After twenty-five, forget it. Dump city." Diane had large breasts herself, but didn't take this as an insult. Miriam couldn't know just how large they were, not from those uniforms they were forced to wear at the nursing home, and they hadn't really seen one another outside of work until tonight. She felt a bit wicked looking at all those naked women, discussing their curves and such. What different worlds she and Miriam lived in. She wasn't sure if it was actually exciting or just interesting. For the moment it didn't matter. "Do you want to see mine?" Miriam asked Diane.

"Your what?" Diane truly didn't know what she meant.

"My breasts, of course. Do you want to compare?"

"No. At least not tonight." Diane wanted to hurt Miriam just a little bit and added, "I've got a lot on my mind. I'm trying to decide which scholarship to accept. I have offers from five universities."

And Miriam felt the blow. She asked her guest if she would like some Sloe Gin and Diane felt forced to accept.

When Miriam was in the kitchen, Diane looked around the room and realized that she could never be friends with this sad loser. She was already planning her escape and how she would distance herself now. She might have to quit the job at the nursing home. She didn't need it really. It was just something she did so her family would say what a hard worker she was. She could find something else to satisfy those purposes.

Diane looked at her watch and sipped the horribly sweet drink. Miriam was thumbing through one of the magazines. Occasionally she traced the outline of a centerfold's breast. Just as Diane was working up an excuse to leave, there was a sound in the other room. Miriam looked at Diane and put her finger to her lips, "Shhh." Miriam slipped off her shoes and tiptoed over to turn off the light-switch. Diane had no idea what was going on, but she was uneasy and regretted she had not made her move to leave.

Miriam was asking her to play along in this private game of hers. She scooted across the floor and pressed her ear against the closed door separating her bedroom from the living room, quietly insisting that Diane do the same. She was smiling gleefully. Diane could barely make out the voices in the living room, but she assumed one of them to be Miriam's mother, Greta. What she heard mostly were grunts and snorts. The man wanted more whiskey. Greta was knocking about in the kitchen, coughing and spitting.

The girls sat like this in the darkness for what felt like fifteen or twenty more minutes, until Miriam finally stood up and flung open the door. Diane was never so embarrassed in her life. The two old people were sitting on the edge of Greta's hide-a-bed. Greta had on only her panties and garter-belt and her nylons rolled down to her ankles, and the old man too still had on his baggy boxer shorts and black socks.

DIANE AND MIRIAM

"What the hell is going on here?" the old man asked. "What kind of goddamned deal is this?"

"Gotcha, didn't I, you old whore," Miriam said with delight.

"I'm sorry, I didn't know," Diane said, imploring forgiveness and glancing at the door. "I really must ..."

"You filthy cunt," the mother said.

LITTLE MAN, WHAT NOW?

At daybreak, I couldn't stand it anymore, and snuck out of bed as quietly as I could without disturbing my wife, Louise. I had been lying awake in there for at least two hours wondering who had won the fight. I had dozed off around six the night before, just as it was heating up. Jeez, how could I doze off like that when I had been waiting for this one so long. It wasn't even a big fight, but I'd had my eye on this kid from Tennessee, Bobby "The Duster" Smith—mean, wiry kid from the hills, probably illiterate, belligerent little bum always says things like, "The pansy will explode when I hit him, they won't be able to find his petals ..." I like that, I like that kid. He's only had five professional fights, all KO's, but he had another 65 amateur fights, Golden Gloves, and he never lost one of them. Then there's this other guy from Newark, a black, calls himself Leroy "The Blender" Saxon. Very mean, himself. He has done time in prison, says he will make hillbilly soup out of Smith. I don't know how I get so fascinated by these guys. My life, or most of our lives, just seem so ordinary, somebody calling himself "The Duster" or "The Blender" brightens my day. But then I had to go and fall asleep just as it looked like these guys were going to hurt each other seriously, you know what I mean?

So I'd been lying there in bed counting Louise's revolutions per hour—she was averaging about 12 per last night, a slow one for her—and wondering just which one of these boys had it in him to do some serious damage to the other. I was also thinking about how selling real estate isn't a proper job for a man, and how I've given twelve of the best years of my life to it, and I feel pretty degraded most of the time, trying to smile, pretending interest in sewage systems, hot water heaters, school zoning—the whole ball of wax, when I don't care, I don't care at all. I just want the miserable, frightened, cautious, impossible-to-please couples to get off their damned rocking horses and let me have my little slice of the pie so Louise can buy her new dishwasher, and, come Christmas, drag me down to her parents' condo in Paradise View, Florida, where the only view is another condo, and her parents can nag away at me for not taking Louise on a shopping spree at the local mall, which should be renamed Mall of the Living Dead—I said that last year and they didn't speak to me until after New Year's. George and Arlene, they live for bowling and miniature golf and Canasta, not even real golf or Bridge. And they are terrible bowlers. What can I say? My two weeks, their only daughter, only child, Louise.

Louise doesn't even know I have this thing for boxing. How would she know, she goes to bed at nine every night. She has the humidifier going full-blast in the bedroom, and I have my little radio out in the kitchen. I turn it on and that's it, I'm in another world. To hell with whether or not the Ramseys will go for the three-bedroom ranch, who needs the Ramseys—what do they think they are, anyway, Egyptian gods! They treat me like I was some lying, sniveling servant just caught stealing spoons. To hell with them. I am now in the dark underworld where "The

Duster" and "The Blender" dance and jab and punch to victory and fame or to pain and defeat, gladiators in a capitalist world of blood and greed. The radio is turned down low and my ear is pushed up right against its tiny speaker, but I am there, and I punch the air and shout silently. How could I have fallen asleep in the sixth round? It's impossible to conceive. Maybe I was KO'd. But by whom? By "The Duster?" By "The Blender?" By the Ramseys? Or could it have been Louise, could Louise have snuck up behind me and with one beautiful round-house punch lifted me right out of my chair? She finally figured out what I was up to all these years?

Anyway, it's embarrassing, but only to myself and to that for which I stand—what the hell does that mean—what does it mean to stand for pressing your ear against a tiny radio speaker on the kitchen table—something, something. I want to know which one of these mean gladiators was hungriest, wanted it the most. Louise is still sleeping. I turn the radio dial, the news, the weather, pop song, pop song, country western, evangelist, stock market, farm report, basketball scores—I pause there—more basketball scores, these people are obsessed with basketball scores, Villanova, Missouri, Georgetown, I don't care, basketball is not my life.

No one, it seems, is the least bit interested in "The Duster" and "The Blender." I can't believe it, two very promising young fighters, one of them may one day have a shot at the title, and no one cares. I'm feeling frantic. I will not meet the Ramseys until I know who prevailed and who tasted humiliation. The appointment with the Ramseys is at nine. Why must my life be tyrannized by details like that. The Ramseys should be forced to live in a cave for at least the next three years for the way they've treated me.

It occurs to me that the News Stand will open in half-an-hour and that, with luck, one of the damned papers should carry the story, though I also fear that the fight didn't end until late, perhaps too late, to get the copy written and fitted in. I'm figuring it will be close, whether or not they got the story in the early edition, very close, and, if not, I cannot see the Ramsey's, that's all there is to that, I cannot face the Ramseys with all their trivial questions aimed at me as if the world depended on my answers: "Yes, there are French doors to the laundry room, but Bobby "The Duster" Smith could walk right through them . . ."

I arrive at the News Stand just as the young girl is opening. There's nothing particularly strange about this, I think to myself, a lot of people want a paper first thing in the morning. I mean, I've never before been there waiting when the person just opened up, but she doesn't know this, no one's keeping score, at least not on me. I stand there at the rack going through three or four different papers with no success. They don't even say, "There was this fight but we had to go to press before the reporter could finish typing his story." It's amazing to me. It's as if this fight never took place. This thought causes me to pause. Is it possible, old boy, that you are losing it? That you dreamed up the whole thing, including every blow of those first six rounds? No, in fact, it is not possible, because, as I said earlier, I had been anticipating this very fight, "The Duster" vs. "The Blender," since I first heard about it more than three weeks ago. I'd read all about them.

The girl behind the counter was watching me, and I knew it and felt a bit self-conscious about going through all these papers and then placing them back in the rack.

"I'm looking for the results of a fight that took place late last night." I said to her, which was true, I wasn't lying or hiding something. "Probably ended about 11:30," I added, for verisimilitude.

"It won't be in any of them," she said, quite civilly I thought, even intelligently. It was a matter-of-fact kind of comment, but backed by confidence, knowledge and experience, despite her youth. And I felt calmly disappointed. She was right. I was sure of it.

"It won't make it until the afternoon edition," she added with a stroke of encouragement. "Which fight, the Smith-Saxon fight?"

"Yes," I said. "Smith-Saxon, that's the one. Do you know?"

"T.K.O. in the 10th. Saxon won. It was incredible; Smith's left eye got opened up in the 7th and Saxon just kept hammering away at it until Smith couldn't see. But Smith was courageous. He'll be back. He looked real good until he got cut."

"Thanks," I said. "I'll be back for the afternoon edition." I started to walk away, but something was nagging at me, something I didn't recognize and had no name for, I stood there on the sidewalk gazing at the morning traffic without really taking it in, without any clear thought at all. A breeze nipped at my ear, and I turned and walked back to the counter.

"I have another question for you," I announced, looking her straight in the eyes. She was a funny looking girl, maybe twenty years old.

She was breaking rolls of dimes on the edge of the cash register. "Yes. And what is that?"

A crazy kind of smile began to spread across my face, I could feel it, and it was utterly new, and I said, "Will you go to Egypt with me?"

SUITE 1306

Ginger had agreed to have a drink with that hairy, fat sales rep from Parkers, Herb what's-his-name, first, because she had already refused him on at least five previous occasions, and she couldn't risk losing the account—he was that type, he would take his business elsewhere—and, well, Michael had called and cancelled their date to go dancing, he was going to his mother's, birthday, something, she hadn't really listened to his explanation after first catching the drift. Michael was not to be counted on these days, she seemed to be last on his list of priorities ever since she had declined his marriage proposal. She didn't want to marry, once was enough, thank you. She wanted to have a good time.

Staying at the Plaza was fun. She mingled easily with the glamorous people in the lobby, French businessmen, heiresses from Palm Beach and Newport, movie stars—Jean Paul Belmondo had tried out his line on her last year, "Have pity on an old man, my child. Let us compromise our lives wantonly!"—and famous writers. Yes, she was a presence in the Oak Room and the Russian Tea Room.

Whether or not management and the bartenders knew it, high-priced hookers worked the room with a panther's grace. Ginger *adored* this part of her cocktail hour after the day's work. She knew their moves, how they followed men out of the room on their way to the rest room downstairs. She knew what the women looked for: out-of-towners, a little tight, with money, vulnerable and randy. Most of the hookers that could make it in The Plaza were extremely beautiful and well-dressed. They could approach a single or a pair of gentlemen without attracting the least bit of attention. And what man, in the city without his wife, would complain to the management that a beautiful woman wanted to share a drink with him? Ginger had never seen one turned away, at least not for a drink. These women fascinated her. She had always meant to strike up a conversation with one.

As she dressed for her drink with hairy Herb she sipped from a glass of wine, washed down a little speed and puffed on a joint of some California sinsemilla her friend Laurie had sent her last week. I mean, she certainly intended to be a little buzzed to get through with this sleaze-bag. Maybe it could even be fun. Why not? Give the guy a bone and leave him sweating. The bar was crowded and she stood there at the entrance surveying the scene. From behind her hands were placed lightly above her hips. “My, aren’t we looking sexy,” he whispered into her ear.

“Nice line, Herb. Cut the shit and find us a table.”

Drinks were ordered, a Margarita for Ginger and a bourbon and water for Herb.

“You know, Ginger, you were magnificent today, a real ball-buster. You made Larry squirm, that’s an achievement.”

“Larry’s a pussywhipped wimp, just like you, Herb. He gave me what I wanted because I let him get a peek up my shirt. Saved me major bucks and he went home happy.”

SUITE 1306

"If it's money you're interested in, sweetie, I could get into that."

Ginger smiled, her cruelest, sexiest, as though that were not out of the realm of possibility. Herb sipped at his drink through a straw and looked up at her. She was looking mean tonight, flecked blond hair, green eyes lit with mischief. Proud and desperate to be whatever it was she was.

"Ginger, I know you think I'm some kind of . . . greaseball . . . salesman, but I've got a heart, too, and I, well, I think you're one of the most attractive women I've ever met." Herb sported muttonchops and a plaid wool tie; he was married to someone even more overweight than himself, and there was little love lost between them.

"I don't think you're a greaseball, Herb. You just leer a lot. You know what I mean by 'leer,' Herb? A woman knows what's on your mind. When we're supposed to be talking prices, you're actually thinking 'pussy,' you're thinking 'tits,' you're thinking you'd like nothing better than to stick your dick in my mouth. A woman knows these things, Herb. You're not as subtle as you'd like to think."

Herb was blushing now, speechless to hear Ginger use words like that. It excited him terribly, but it was also embarrassing. Hookers talked like that. He paid them to talk that way, but not attractive, respectable businesswomen, at least not in his experience.

"Well, it is true that I've had fantasies about you . . ." He sipped at his drink, unable to meet her sadistic gaze. Why had it started off like this? This wasn't how he had imagined their "date." He wanted to impress her with his considerate, tender, curious, witty charms. He knew she thought him to be coarse, coarser than the fashionable, younger people he imagined her dancing with after meetings when she came to town.

"Let's hear them, tell me your fantasies about me." Ginger's head was fairly spinning with the mixture of the tequila and speed and sinsemilla. She was having a surprisingly good time making Herb squirm. She ordered another round from the waitress.

"No, Ginger, let's talk about something else. I didn't mean for it to be like this, honestly. I wanted you to . . . like me. I wanted to make you laugh."

"But I am laughing, Herb. You said you'd had fantasies about me. I'm just curious. Was I good? Did you do anything weird to me, Herb? Because I'm not into being tied up or, you know, whips or anything."

"There was nothing like that, Ginger, I promise you. It's just that . . . No, I can't say it. Tell me about your house in Connecticut." He was sweating now. Herb always sweated. His chin was permanently pressed against his chest now. He made eye contact with Ginger only furtively now and then, knowing that she was mocking him.

"Herb, you're being an ass now. Come on, I want to hear what you do to me in your dreams. Anything involving chocolate or electric appliances? Tell me, I'm flattered. You'll cheer me up if you tell me. Otherwise, this is going to be a dull evening, okay?"

"It's nothing special, Ginger."

"Nothing special ? Well, thanks a lot! That takes the cake!"

"No, I didn't mean it like that. You know what I mean. I mean, we just do it, very romantically, very slowly, tenderly, and it's . . . it's beautiful and . . ."

"And what, Herb? And what?" "And well, you know."

"No, I don't know, Herb. It's your fantasy, I don't know."

"And you tell me I'm the best you've ever had. That's all."

"Ginger couldn't constrain herself now and burst out laughing. Of all the fantasies he might have confessed, this one struck her as the funniest. "You're really something else, Herb. You know that?"

"I'm sorry, Ginger. Really I am. Forgive me." He reached across the table tentatively and took her hand in his. He knew his was damp and he wasn't entirely in control. Ginger was repulsed at first, but then realized what she had done. She had lured him into her trap, and had forced him into it, and then mocked him savagely.

"It was a sweet fantasy, Herb. I don't know what made me laugh, I'm sorry."

They sat there in silence holding hands across the table. Ginger had spent her venom for the moment. Herb's confidence was slowly coming back to him. He even allowed himself to think: *I've got her where I want her now.*

"So what do you think, babe, shall we have one more round? You're already home, just take the elevator to bed. How's your room, by the way? Got a view this time?"

Ginger withdrew her hand slowly and finished her drink. "Sure, why not? Let's have another. The room's great, you know, magic fingers and soft porn on the cable. I could live in this hotel. Great room service, all these sexy Italian bellhops."

"You're too much, Ginger, you know that? If you were mine I'd give you anything in the world. Honest, I would. Nothing would be too much for you."

Ginger smiled. "How much for one night?" she said. She hadn't really meant to say it, it just leapt out automatically under her breath.

"What did you say?"

"I said, how much for one night? How much would you pay to, uh, have your way with me?"

Herb sat up straight now, the first time since sitting down. He looked her straight in the eyes. Was she starting up the game again? Was she mocking?

"You're not serious."

"Oh, I'm serious, Herb. I want to know, how much for one evening, straight, nothing weird, how much would you pay me?"

He was scratching his head and pulling at his muttonchops. "I don't know, I'd have to think about it. You're not serious?"

"Herb, you said if I was yours nothing would be too much. So I just want to know how much it would be worth to you to have me for one night."

"Maybe three hundred. How does three hundred sound? That's more than these girls get," he looked around the room and, sure enough, there were at least three girls working the room right then.

"Yeah, but I'm not a hooker, Herb. I'm me, your fantasy girl.

You know I'd never fuck you without some special incentive. Three hundred's chicken feed. I wouldn't let you squeeze my left tit for three hundred."

Herb was puzzled now. Every time he made an effort to get the conversation on to something other than sex, this incredibly beautiful, younger businesswoman worked it back to dirty talk. "How much?" she repeated. "How much would you pay, Herb?"

"Well, I'm maybe not as rich as I let on. I don't know, I guess I could come up with five, six hundred."

"For six hundred I'll dance naked for you but no touching, nothing." Jesus Christ, Herb thought to himself, this woman is serious. She must be loaded. And then he thought, why not? Go for it. Fuck this dame, just plain fuck this beautiful dame because I am never going to have another chance.

"A thousand," he said. "A thousand for the night, and that's my last offer."

"Let's go," she said.

If rooms could talk, if Suite 1306 could tell its long, jagged story. At eight o'clock on this particular Monday evening, a shapely blond woman with green eyes undressed before a perspiring middle-aged overweight man. Neither spoke. The caustic jibes had ceased in the elevator. Now Ginger's hands shook as she removed each article of clothing. Herb sat on the edge of the bed tapping the fingers of his hands together. Then she tossed her sheer bikini panties over her shoulder and said, "There." It was all done. She had had her appendix removed, he noticed that first.

Herb *was* a gentle lover. He never took his eyes off hers for the four hours they were in bed together. And he spoke only to ask if this was good, if this pleased her. And she said yes, yes, as if in a dream.

Michael called from the lobby around nine the next morning. In her room they shared a breakfast of cafe au lait and croissants with butter and jam. It really had been his mother's birthday and he was sorry to have cancelled their plans. She told him she had stayed in and watched a movie on TV. She was hoping he would ask her to marry him again. She even thought of telling him that a man had offered her a thousand dollars for one night. Think of the money that he, Michael, would be saving in a lifetime of thousand-dollar nights. Suddenly, with no warning, she started to cry.

A WINDOW OF SOCIABILITY

Maxine and I had been married for over a year before I finally met her brother, Todd. It was a second marriage for both of us and we hadn't invited family to the ceremony. Still, in the course of the first year we had more than made it up to her parents, inviting them over to dinner at least once a month, taking them to concerts on the green in the summer. It's not as though Todd lived in Baghdad or something—he wasn't more than three miles across town. And he was my age, too, which for some reason made it even more of a curiosity.

I spoke to him on the phone a number of times, and he seemed like a pretty exciting guy to me, the kind of guy that is always stumbling into the center of the action. Just this year alone he was in the bank when it was robbed—one of the masked bandits even took a shot at him when he tried to trip the alarm—and he was in the disco the night it burned down. His accounts of these calamities and others never fail to rivet me, my life pales in comparison, as they say. But Maxine barely responds when I tell her of one of Todd's adventures, and she never invites him over and we never visit him at his place. Todd keeps saying he will have me over, soon as he can find "a window of sociability." That always cracks me up. He's some kind of inventor, and that interests me a lot also. I think I know the type—brilliant, obsessed, but chaotic, the house always a mess with little mechanical parts spread everywhere. Of course he could never get it together to throw a proper dinner party, and maybe even his own family thinks he doesn't have time for them, maybe they're hurt. But he sounds like somebody I would like, I would probably forgive him his eccentricities and find his obsessions very interesting.

Maxine really annoys me sometimes when I try to get her to talk about Todd. "His life's his own," she says, which is a very unsatisfying response. I don't even know if he was ever married, things that basic. It's true that when he calls he barely asks about Maxine. He will say "How's Max?" but it's clear in his tone that he doesn't want a whole long story and will usually cut me off if I start one. "Gotta rush, something's about to explode." Every family has its mysteries and squabbles, I figure it's just a temporary thing. But I didn't have many friends, and I already liked Todd, as I said before, just from our phone conversations. I could use somebody exciting like that in my life, not that I was unhappy. Our marriage had so quickly fallen into place that it felt as if we had always been married, which was good, but still I hadn't been out without Maxine even once in the whole year.

I decided to take the initiative, even if it might be awkward at first, and just drop in on Todd at his place. I didn't mention Todd in the note I left for Maxine on the kitchen counter, just "Won't be home until late. I'll get something to eat out. Love—."

"Todd." I said, "I'm Jake. Thought I'd break the ice . . ."

He looked mildly surprised, but put me at my ease right away. "Come in, come in, I've been meaning to . . . Hey, glad you came."

He turned off the television and invited me to have a seat, served me some iced tea, and we were off, like old friends.

"Jesus, Jake, I've got to tell you the damndest thing just happened to me. I was in the supermarket this afternoon, you know, sizing up some produce, polishing a couple of tomatoes, when this incredibly beautiful woman comes up to me and says. I swear it, she says to me, looking me right in the eyes, she says "I can polish better than that." And she invites me over to her place and, I swear, I have never been seduced like that in my life. This woman does a striptease for me that would have popped your eyes right out of your head. Jesus, was she built. And she did it all, you know what I mean, *all* and more."

"You're kidding me? Today?" I didn't know he was a ladies man on top of everything else.

"Yeah, I just got home an hour ago. Marathon, you know what I mean?"

"Sure, of course I do. A complete stranger, never seen her before in your life?"

"That's right. She was rich, too, I can tell you that. Whirlpool bath, champagne, she drives a black Jaguar. It's not the first time I've been picked up in a supermarket, mind you, but today was the best." I looked around his little bachelor bungalow. It wasn't nearly as cluttered and chaotic as I had expected. In fact, it was pretty plain, a high school debate team plaque was propped up on the mantle next to a dime-store picture of The Fonz.

"When I was in Nam . . ."

"You were in Viet Nam? Maxine never . . ."

"Oh yeah. Special Forces. I was at Ashair when it was overrun in '65. That was some bad shit, let me tell you. I lost twenty-six buddies in two days. 'One more GI from Vietnam, St. Peter; I've served my time in hell . . .' That was some bad shit. In a monsoon, man, you know what I mean? The place was one blazing ammo dump. I didn't know who I was shooting at. You just squeezed the trigger and kept on squeezing 'til you woke up dead or alive *somewhere*. They cleaned our clocks."

I didn't know what to say but I was fairly certain therein lay the secret to the distant relations with the members of his family. I couldn't help but sympathize with Todd, even though I sat that war out in college and felt a little guilty now. I've got nearly perfect relations with his parents and his sister and he can't see them. It really broke my heart to think of what must go through his dreams at night. "Maxine never told . . ."

"Oh you know women. She wants to pretend it never happened. You say Bien Hoa to her, you say Bong-son, An-Khe, she thinks you're ordering Chinese food. You say Death before Dishonor and she thinks you're taking a nap before dinner. What do they know? Tell me that, huh, what do they know?"

"And what about your father, can't you talk to him at least?"

"My father thinks I should sell new cars, just like him. Don't worry about it, Jake. I'm doing all right. Hey, look on the bright side. What about today, huh, what about that beautiful broad today? My life isn't so bad, it just isn't what *they* want it to be. So to hell with them is what I say. I've got my own life."

"I wanted to ask you about that, about what you're working on now."

"It's top-secret for the moment. But when the patent comes through you'll be the first to know, Jake. You're okay, you know that. You're okay. I think I'm going to strike it big on this one, and maybe I'll even let you in on a piece of the action. There should be enough for everybody. The folks will stop griping then, you wait and see. Money, the great healer, right?"

"I suppose so, Todd. I'm sure everything will change when they see what you've been up to. I think you're just a bit of a mystery to them, that's my opinion."

"Say, you want to watch a *Kojak* re-run with me? It's on in a couple of minutes."

"Thanks anyway, Todd, but Maxine will be wondering where the hell I am."

"Women. Sure. Hey, thanks for dropping by. It's about time."

"Yeah, let's stay in touch, buddy."

When I got home I couldn't help it, I was really mad at Maxine. "Give the guy a break," I said, "after what he's been through."

"What the hell are you talking about," she said.

"I mean, it's a miracle the guy's alive and you and your damned parents can't even treat him as if . . ."

"Just what in the hell are you talking about, Mr. Know-it-all?"

"Christ, Maxine, have you ever been shot at? Have you ever had twenty-six of your buddies killed? What do you think I'm talking about?"

"Frankly, my dear, I haven't a notion of what you are referring to. Is this something to do with Todd? What did that asshole tell you to get you so riled up?"

"Vietnam, for Christ's sake, what the hell do you think I'm talking about?"

"Todd? Are you out of your mind?"

"Yes, Todd, in Vietnam, what do you think . . . ?"

And that's when Maxine started to laugh. She laughed doubled over, clutching her stomach. "Todd? Vietnam?" She couldn't stop laughing long enough to talk. I was completely confused as to what was going on now.

"Stop laughing, damn it. Stop it."

"Oh you poor boy, you poor, stupid boy."

"Stop it. What are you talking about? Stop it now, damn it."

She tried to stop, she put her hand over her mouth, but squeaks and howls continued for another minute until I forced her to sit down and talk straight to me.

"Come on, what's going on now, you can't do this to me."

"The closest Todd ever got to Vietnam was Boston. You *actually* believed him? I can't believe it."

"Todd wasn't in Vietnam? Are you kidding me? Why would he tell me that whole story of 26 buddies . . . ?"

"Todd has never done *anything*, get it through your head. He's a pathological liar, a completely pathological liar. It started when he was very young. He's an extremely lazy and boring person, that's a terrible thing to say about one's brother, but it's true. We've just given up on him, we don't talk about him because there's nothing to say, except that he lies and never does anything."

"Then that woman today at the supermarket . . ."

"Woman? Are you crazy? The little twerp is a virgin, I'll swear to that."

"He just sits in there and watches television?"

"You got it, buster. That's the complete picture. He's just boring and he lies to cover it up. But nobody believes anything he says, nobody but you."

I thought about this last utterance of Maxine's. I thought

about it all night. In fact, I couldn't sleep. I kept dreaming of the raid on Ashair, all that pain and gore, but then I would switch and think about that incredibly sexy lady at the supermarket, "I can polish better than that," she said, over and over. It was not such a bad life, and I liked Todd better than ever. He fascinated me, and I wanted to get to know him.

HER LIFE'S ADVENTURE

Alexandra Huntington—known to her friends as Alex—was a painter whose specialty was nude self-portraits. At thirty-nine she was still a handsome woman, dark, of medium height, thin-boned without an extra ounce of meat. Having never been married, she had a lot of thoughts about herself. Despite her olive skin, she was pure-bred British upper-class. She was widely traveled, at home in Paris or Rome or, indeed, Tanzania. And she was a woman of ideas. Many of her lovers had been writers and intellectuals, professors, and she prided herself on picking up at least one good idea from every affair. She could talk for ten minutes on any number of lofty subjects.

More than a few of Alex's affairs had been with married men. And in her own analysis, she had comported herself with the utmost sophistication and moral equanimity. Her solution in each case was to make friends with the wife, to be as open, gentle and non-threatening as possible. The wives would quickly discover in her a true friend, one who did not want to steal their husbands, just borrow them from time to time. In fact, more often than not, after several months of vigorous sexual use, the friendship with the wife would begin to take precedence over the borrowing of the husband. Then, inevitably, there was the question of the next step: should the two women actually make love with one another, even though neither was lesbian by nature. By the time this question had arisen, the husband had usually moved on to a new mistress, and was just as happy to let the women forget him and pass the time solving their own quandary.

So, in a sense, she was attaching herself to families. Often there were children, and Alex gladly accepted the role of surrogate mother. She took the children on outings to museums and zoos, bought gifts of clothing for them. Their real mothers couldn't help but be grateful. She would become a known figure, an important family friend, to all the in-laws. A few might have suspected an unusual arrangement, this attractive woman always visiting, never married herself; but Alex would soon have them charmed into trusting her as if she were a real family member.

When she did return to her own apartment her first action was to undress and stand before her mirrors—she had several arranged in a half-circle—and study her body from as many angles as possible. Her absorption in the examination would increase as she poured herself numerous glasses of scotch. She held her breasts with both hands and seemed lost in a trance, oblivious to time. Would Time sneak up behind and ravage her? Was she immune? Was she an exception? She liked to flirt with these thoughts but had ways of escaping them if they became too grim. Her paintings hinted at these dark thoughts, she liked to think. Their intention was far more than to capture fleeting beauty, she was a deeper person than that.

One affair that haunted her, that raised certain questions about her character, was with a Hungarian violinist in Toronto. He was married and had a family, but they were back in Budapest, and so there was no question of a menace. Emil was an eager and imaginative lover, and Alex immediately felt he had been created especially for her. They made love at least twice a day in the first months of their relationship. She went to all his concerts and sat in the audience with pride and lust in her heart, knowing he found her desirable and worthy of his hands, his mouth, his whole body and mind. She would even secretly arouse herself during the concert, and experienced orgasms on more than one occasion. This was the life she had been preparing for herself all along: Culture, good looks, and continual sexual satisfaction, even ecstasy.

One night, after making love, she told Emil about the orgasms she experienced watching him perform in the concert hall. "Really," he said, "just watching me? I must be very good. Perhaps you aren't the only woman in the audience experiencing these climaxes. Did you ever think of that?" And then he bit her neck, and they wrestled in the sheets until they both desired to make love again.

This was without question the happiest time in her life. She did several life-size canvases of Emil in the nude. They joked. He requested a larger penis, and she obliged. He suggested she make his tongue into a lascivious serpent in honor of his superb cunnilingus technique, and she, with delight and laughter, again complied. And the hands, the hands should be as soft and sensual as velvet or silk, in honor of the endless pleasures they had given to every inch of her olive skin.

But then something unimaginably tragic occurred, something even too hideous and ironic for novels or cinema. It was a night in February, the coldest of the year. The apartment was cold.

They had called the landlord and he had said he was doing everything he could, but repairmen were on call and it would be several hours before he could promise more heat. Alex and Emil had made love once, but they were still cold. They had lit candles and warmed their hands over the flames. They had drunk one bottle of wine between them, but Emil wanted more, or better yet, he wanted cognac. Alex told him he was a fool if he thought he was going out into the freezing night air just for a bottle of cognac. But, secretly, it was an example of what she loved most in him, his impetuosity, and so she let him go.

But he was gone for more than an hour. The city was dark and there was no traffic and certainly no pedestrians. He had found the liquor store, some eight blocks from their apartment, but had somehow gotten lost on the way back. Not badly lost, just a wrong turn that took him several blocks in the wrong direction. The air burned the skin, burned it as if a blow-torch was aimed at him just inches away. He hurried, thought of Alex, thought most of all of the cognac, how good it would feel.

Alex threw her arms around him when he finally opened the door. "My god, I was worried. Quick, get your shoes off. Put this blanket around you." She tried to warm him up as fast as possible. Emil joked and demanded a large tumbler of cognac.

They woke the next morning with sizable hangovers, having finished the entire bottle. Neither could remember the end of the evening. Emil had a rehearsal at ten and Alex planned to stay home and paint as it was still way below zero outside.

Around 10:30 the phone rang. It was Emil, he sounded strange and had trouble speaking. "Something's wrong," he said over and over, and then couldn't find words to describe what it was that was wrong. "I have to come home, I'll be home in half-an-hour." "Okay, I'll be here. Emil, what is it? Can't you tell me what it is?"

She had never seen him so dispirited. He paced the apartment, rubbing his hands together, unable to speak. "Are you sick?" she asked. "Do you want something for your stomach? Is that it? Are you still hungover?" But he was remote from her; for the first time since they had met she couldn't reach him. He responded to none of her usual ploys.

Finally his nerves exhausted him and he crawled into bed and pulled the blankets up to his chin. Alex sat nearby in a chair and stared at his face, his whole head really, and then she herself began to have terrible thoughts: at odd moments, his head weakly rolled to the side, Emil resembled John Keats on his deathbed as painted by Walter Severn.

About five o'clock that afternoon she called a doctor-friend of Emil's, a Hungarian emigrant by the name of Otto Pick. She told his secretary that it was an emergency.

Otto arrived at the apartment a little after six, his concern for their emergency could be seen in his demeanor. Usually a friend of quick wit and immense charm, he now moved to Emil's bedside and spoke in almost hushed tones. Alex could tell him only of Emil's return from rehearsal, his nervous pacing, his unwillingness to tell her what was wrong.

The doctor pulled back the blankets and began to probe Emil's abdominal area gently. He, with Alex's help, removed Emil's trousers and shirt.

"I am taking him to the hospital now. I want to give him some tests." He would tell her nothing more.

The two of them helped Emil down the stairs and into the backseat of Otto's Mercedes Benz.

Emil the violinist, Emil the lover, Emil the *bon vivant*, had seven fingers and four toes amputated the next day, a victim of frostbite. Alex was at the hospital every minute permitted. She herself was in shock, and Otto insisted she take strong tranquillizers. Still, she chain-smoked, and stared ahead at the white walls with sickness in her heart.

Emil was permitted to return home six days later, feet and hands bandaged thickly. Alex made soups for him. He wouldn't talk so she began to read to him, first from *The Magic Mountain*, his favorite novel, but it was too depressing and she switched to *Growth of the Soil*. It was a sober, long-winded book, with no flash of comedy. And when Emil slept, she tried to imagine their life together. Everyday, as the days went on, she spent two or three hours daydreaming about what their life would be. Emil, most obviously, would never play again. But also—and this at first pained her unbearably to even think, and she hated herself for allowing such a selfish thought to even occur to her—never again would he twirl her nipples sensuously between his thumb and finger. And more. And more. Most likely, he would never again be the light-hearted, impetuous lover and gentleman she had known during these past months. O how it hurt to allow these thoughts to surface. How selfish!

After several weeks Emil had his bandages removed, and the sight was hard to bear for both of them. Alex feigned good cheer, and to her surprise Emil began to joke about taking up the ukulele, playing on streetcorners to support them. He even wanted to make love again, but during the course of their love-making Alex's heart locked shut and she knew it was now only a matter of finding the least hurtful moment to leave, to leave Emil but also Toronto. This chapter was closed.

She was lucky to find a job teaching painting at a small women's college in New England. After six years, she was awarded tenure. Only now and then, when she is getting to know someone new and trying to convey an essence of what her life adventure has been to this point, will she make reference to those extraordinary months with Emil in Toronto. She usually concludes the anecdote by saying, "But of course I had to leave him then, I'm such a sensual person."

VACATION

Rita and I had just driven 120 miles for no reason. We had bought some lawn ornaments from an Asian lady who had warned us that people often shot the bears because they were so realistic. And we had also purchased some very tiny lawn furniture, though we didn't own children, it was just an inspired idea.

We stopped at Dot's Restaurant and ordered some Jailhouse Chili, it had won first place for taste and presentation the year before. I'm not entirely sure what the waitress meant by presentation. It had a sprig of parsley on it or something, a maraschino cherry. Maybe the woman who served it was nude.

"And I'll have a glass of iced tea," I added.

"No iced tea," the waitress told me. She was cute and had a Long Island accent. We were far from Long Island.

"It's iced tea season," I said.

"We're not serving it because the town water stinks. No one's drunk water here for five months."

"Busted pipe?" I inquired.

"Dead bird," she replied, walking away.

There was an enormous fat guy seated at the counter. He was about seventy years old and was missing every other tooth. His face had been carved out of mush with a meat cleaver. He said to the waitress, "How about a ham hock?"

"You wanna fork?" she asked.

"Nah, I'll use my fingers." He popped the tenderloin part into his mouth immediately upon delivery. And then stared at the revolting fat circle for a few moments. There seemed to be a little debate going on in his fat head. Then he threw the whole thing into his mouth and swallowed.

We grinned at him. He was enjoying his life. It was about three o'clock in the afternoon and I figured that all his nutritional needs had been met for this day.

"Rita," I said, "are we in Griswoldville or what?"

Rita bit into a chip and smiled, "Well, it ain't the end of the world but it's as close as we're likely to get."

"You're a poorly conceived character, you know that, Rita?"

"Well, I'm not walking away, if that's what you're getting at. Everything about this place suggests my pre-existence."

Rita had flown up from Oklahoma and was about the size of a lawn ornament, a big one. People were always taking shots at her, but she wasn't shy of shooting back. Once she stabbed a raccoon to death for just looking at her.

I was on vacation.

When we left Dot's I told the waitress we'd be back, but that was a lie. There are a lot of places that just don't merit a return. Dead bird, my ass.

We looked at the map for a good long time. "Ever been to Marlboro?" Rita finally asked me.

"No, but I have a Marlboro beach towel."

"Then let's go."

She threw the map out the window. "It just gets in the way," she explained. I knew what she meant. The Asian lady who had sold us the bear had referred to Rita as my wife. She said, "You and your wife might like that." We were comfortable with that, even though Rita was a little lesbian. She wasn't very lesbian, and yet she was only lesbian. I barely know what I'm talking about.

It was a great day for driving fast and turning up the volume on the radio. We stopped at several junk shops and bought stuff we didn't need. It was important to touch base with the people, to see if they had any thoughts about the world's decline or new products. Most of them seemed to be surprisingly happy. I really was surprised. Even relieved, I guess you could say. Even the people in trailers waved to us. We stopped at a phone booth and Rita called some girl in Norman, Oklahoma to tell her she wanted to have her baby or something.

Marlboro wasn't much of a town, two churches, a gas station, a couple of kids on bicycles, an old guy leaning on a tree. There was one tiny shop called The Other Shop with a closed sign on the door. We parked the car and walked around for a half-an-hour looking for the other shop, but there didn't seem to be one. I guess that's what you might call an excellent example of desperate small town humor. Rita and I were holding hands and probably looked to the natives as if we were thinking of settling down here, and maybe even opening a shop. It wasn't entirely out of the question, at least as far as I was concerned.

"But you can't get a drink in this metropolis," Rita noticed.

"You're a genius," I said. "What was I thinking? You also can't get a meal, you can't get laid, you can't buy a book or a record or a pair of socks. This is the end of the world, a little patch of nothingness for people who don't care enough to bother. Would you care to interview anyone before we motivate on out of here back into the zone of engagement?"

The gas station attendant had been staring at us for a while. Rita lifted her shirt and flashed her tits at him. He waved back.

I love to vacation with Rita. She's so affirmative. So zesty.

Five days later we stopped in a place called Buckland and ordered chocolate malts. We both had the hots for our waitress. Her name was Nadine and she was about six foot three. She looked like she could find herself around an aisle full of cleaning products real handily.

"You'd disappear in her," I told Rita rather cruelly. "She's more my type."

"I bet she threw the javelin in high school," Rita said.

"That suits me just fine," I said. "Useful."

"What?"

"I mean, if I get laid off. At work. She could throw the javelin."

"Frieda pole-vaulted to glory," Rita said.

"Who the hell is Frieda?" I asked. Nadine really was about the size of a totem pole, but she had a much better figure. She looked like Jayne Mansfield on stilts, except she wasn't a bleached blond.

Actually she doesn't look like Jayne Mansfield at all. That was a hasty and inaccurate cheap little simile entirely inappropriate. She looks like Connie Chung on stilts, except that she isn't Asian, even marginally. She was born and bred in Buckland. What does that mean, bred? Did they actually breed her? I know I would like to be her stud. Rita has always called me "Spud." She knows

I don't much like it, and that I would rather be a Stud, Nadine's own personal Stud, as it turns out, for now, at least, while we founder awhile here in Buckland.

"Frieda is my girlfriend in Norman, Spudman, and she is still swimming in glory as the state champ of female pole-vaulting, 1968."

"You could bring her along some time. I'd like to measure her glory."

"She is, uh, disabled."

"Landed on her head one too many times?"

"That's pretty much Frieda's story."

"But I bet her mind is as sharp as a pin, right?"

"Not exactly," Rita said, watching Nadine bend over to pick up a spoon.

"Why don't you throw your napkin on the floor and see if she'll pick it up. We could get a glimpse of her tits, maybe. I'm on vacation, you know. I deserve something."

"It's my vacation, too, Spuddy. I'm a human being."

"No, you're not. You're more like a lima bean. Now Nadine is more like a human being. Or more, she's ten human beings and three or four angels and a cheetah all wrapped up in one delicious body. She's a celestial zoo and a vast box of animal crackers."

A couple of days later we were in Conway. Rita had to call Frieda about something. Frieda was supposed to feed Rita's cats. But Frieda never remembered. I eavesdropped this time. I was interested in how you talked to someone swimming in glory and out of their mind.

VACATION

"Just let them out," Rita insisted. "They've got little dining-out cards around their necks and can receive free meals at a variety of local pet restaurants. I'll be back in a couple of days. You hang in there, sweetheart. I'll bring you lots of presents. Yes, Rome was crowded and noisy and Venice was completely washed away, but we had fun anyway. We fished for ancient busts and got lucky. You'll see. No, we didn't watch *Dynasty*, too fuzzy. I love you, too."

When she finished I decided to keep my thoughts to myself. I could have said something, but, then, it wasn't my business.

"This Conway is one big turkey farm," I said. "I counted four truckloads of turkeys drive by in the last two minutes. Have you noticed the feathers just floating around?"

Rita was staring at the stars on her shoes, maybe she was counting them. She looked sad.

"How was Frieda?" I asked.

"I don't think Frieda's going to make it another year, and here I am driving around with you flirting with waitresses all over. I'm a scumbag, Spud. I should be back there making sure she takes her medicine and everything."

"Gee, Rita, I'm sorry. You never even mentioned Frieda to me before."

"Well, we haven't really been an item all that long. And besides, it's a secret in Norman. Dykes are lower than armadillo in Oklahoma, and that's saying something because there are no armadillos in Oklahoma."

We were still just standing there without a clue, but that's how we travel, Rita and I. We try to take a trip like this once a year, just drive every which way and then stop for refreshments and junk. She buys a lot of old hats and costume jewelry, and I buy anything that strikes my fancy. I've known her since she was a pup.

"We're not really lovers, it just feels like it," Rita said.

"I didn't ask, and I didn't presume."

Another convoy of turkey transports chugged by. All these white feathers came floating down on us. I picked a couple out of Rita's hair, then she picked some out of my face.

"This is a sorry little place. Can you imagine spending your life blowing turkey feathers out of your mouth," Rita said, blowing a feather out of her mouth.

"I could use a rum and Coke about now. I know a place over in Shelburne Falls, you can sit by the window, or better yet, out on the deck and look down at the river."

We got back in the car and I kissed Rita lightly on the lips. I'm sorry for what I said about Rita being not much bigger than a lawn ornament.

"Gimme another ham hock," she said.

"Dead bird," I said.

RAVEN OF DAWN

Mitzi was having trouble getting George's attention lately. George was obsessed with the foundation of their house. He would get home from work, change clothes, and go outside immediately. She'd watch him from the kitchen window staring into the hole he had dug over the weekend. He'd stand like that until dark, scratching his head. He didn't talk about it with her, but it seemed as if that hole was the only thing in the world he really cared about.

She talked to her older sister, Lynn, about it.

"Bryan went through a period like that, only with him it was the car. I swear he took that thing apart bolt by bolt until there was nothing left. It lasted about a year."

"And then what happened?" Mitzi asked.

"Nothing dramatic. He just gave up. We had to buy a new car."

"I know that, I remember very well. I mean, did you get his attention back? Did he, uh, come back into the marriage?"

"Honey, Bryan has never been fully here. I just stopped expecting much."

This was not what Mitzi wanted to hear, and she was sorry she had confided her fears to her sister. Lynn drank too much and had a bleak outlook on life. It often seemed to Mitzi that Lynn wanted to drag her down with her. And Mitzi was determined to not follow in her sister's footsteps. George had been, after all, a fine, loving husband for the past four years.

They had friends, they took vacations, he brought her presents and generally considered her happiness above all other concerns. It's just that, as he said to her recently, he's concerned with protecting their investment.

Mitzi had tried all the most obvious tricks recommended by the women's magazines. She had welcomed him home one day dressed in some new sheer lingerie, but she felt ridiculous and quickly changed into her housedress before he could even comment.

"George," she said, "Before you go out there, can't we have a little talk? You haven't had much time for me lately. I know you're concerned with the foundation, but don't you think about anything else? Can't we still have a little fun?"

George looked at her for a long time before speaking. It was as if he were listening to a language he didn't fully understand.

"If I don't get it done before winter," he paused and stroked her hair away from her eyes. "You know, Mitzi, I sometimes wonder if I deserve you. I don't, really. I've had such dark thoughts lately. Sometimes I think I'm some kind of monster, that I should live alone in a forest and live off nuts and berries, and never speak again or see another living being."

"Oh George, I've never heard you talk like this. Is it something I've done?"

He had a tear in his eye but wiped it away quickly.

"You are too good for me. No matter what you say, it's true. I should live in a cave with bats and transparent fish. I'm a blot on the sun."

Mitzi declared her undying love for him. She tried her best to convince him that he was the sweetest and gentlest man she had ever known, but then he pushed her away from him—a gesture entirely foreign to him until that moment—and went back outside and stared into the hole until past nightfall.

"He's too young for male menopause, " her mother told her. "You sure it isn't another woman, or maybe something happened at the office that he's not telling you."

"I don't think so, mother. I used to think he told me everything, that George would never lie to me."

"You should check his drawers, go through his wallet. You'd be surprised what I found out about your father when I searched his wallet. Receipts can tell you a lot. Check his address book too for names not familiar to you. Even good men lead double-lives. Your father had a dozen letters in his office desk from a woman named Olga of whom he never spoke. He had known her for thirty years, apparently. But he was always good to me, I never had a complaint in all our years together. He was generous to a fault. But he had this Olga-thing. It was as if that thing existed on another plane, you know what I mean? As if . . ."

"But mother, that's not what I'm worried about. I'm worried that George might, you know, hurt himself or something. He might just disappear."

"Well, I don't know about that, honey. That's another thing altogether, though you know my friend Marjorie's husband did just that, he disappeared without a trace. She never got so much as a postcard. Everything perfectly normal right up to that day. He even bought her a hat and took her to the movies the day before it happened. I always liked Webb, too. Kind of had a special place for him in my heart, if you know what I mean."

Every time Mitzi mentioned her problem to somebody she came away less reassured than before, so that, increasingly, she had reason to feel threatened by George's distance and the things he would say to her when they did talk.

"Why do you just stand there and stare into that hole, George? It's as if you are watching something in there. Is there something in there, George? Have you got some kind of TV in there, George, because if you do, I wish you'd bring it inside and let me watch it too, because I'll be damned if I'm going to stand out there with you. The neighbors must think you're digging my grave, really. Everybody can see you standing out there night after night. George, it's been months now, and I can't, for the life of me, figure out what's bothering you."

"It's rotten. It's that simple, Mitzi, the entire foundation of our house is rotten."

"I don't care about the house. I care about you, George. You never talk to me anymore."

George couldn't look her in the face now. He would look anywhere to avoid her eyes.

"Why don't you call an expert? We can borrow if we have to. How expensive can it be? Mother would be happy to give us a loan. It's not worth all this grieving that's come between us."

"Do you know what's wrong with you, Mitzi?"

She froze-up at the sound of his voice. He sounded different, like someone she didn't know, someone who was going to hurt her.

"You're too good. You believe everyone is good. You think it's all going to work out. Well, let me tell you something: this house is going to crumble and fall straight through to hell. And you know what you're going to find there?"

"Stop it, George. Stop right there. I'm not going to take this anymore. I've about had it." And he did stop it. He went back outside and stared deep into the hole.

When Mitzi woke the next morning she discovered that George had not come to bed at all last night. The car was gone and there was no note left on the bulletin board. She was frightened, but tried not to panic. Normally she would have called her mother or Lynn, but instinct told her they would only make matters worse. Instead, she thumbed through the telephone book until she found an ad for a foundation contractor.

"It's an emergency," she explained. "I would be really grateful if you could come today. I'd be willing to pay extra."

The man on the other end of the phone agreed to come. He liked her voice, her sense of helplessness appealed to him.

"In all honesty, Mrs. Cook, there's nothing wrong with your foundation. It's solid and dry. I could take your money and spend a week out here poking around, but the results would be the same. You've got no problems here. I ought to know, I laid this foundation twenty years ago. It'll be here when we're long gone. So, enjoy your house. No charge, okay. Your husband is a lucky man."

She almost wanted to say, that's what you think. *My husband is the raven of dawn, the father of lies* . . . But of course she didn't. She thanked the nice man and offered him a piece of coffee cake. She was pretending he was her man. It was a very dangerous game, but suddenly she liked danger. It reminded her of George, wherever he was now.

FRIENDS

Even in our town there is a limit to how much idle talk one can tolerate. My family's been here since the beginning of time, and I think I know a little bit about what happens to people. They fall in love with the right mate or the wrong one, or they don't fall in love at all. They are blessed with a good mind or they are not. Good health or bad health. They believe in God or they don't. And so on. But what I can't stand are those people who stand around on the sidelines chewing on everyone else's fortunes. It's hard enough to get on with one's life without the tittle-tattle of a quidnunc spotlighting your weakness.

Cora Duckworth is the person I have in mind. She comes in my backdoor without knocking at least five days a week. I'm ironing or doing the dishes or vacuuming. I don't want to stop what I'm doing, but eventually she wins out and I put on a pot of coffee.

"I think Elaine is going to have a breakdown if Booker doesn't stop flirting with Becky at the City Cafe. He goes there every day and Becky fills his cup without charging him until Mr. Berry finally tells her he's going to take it out of her pay. Really. Melissa, everyone knows what's going on there, and Elaine just can't take it much longer. Have you seen how she looks? It's a sin."

"I've known Booker all my life, and I can tell you, Cora, he's as harmless as they come. Heck, he's been madly in love with Elaine since he was in the sixth grade. Elaine has nothing to worry about and she knows it. Booker's just got too much time on his hands since he gave up coaching Little League on advice of Doc Edwards."

I was, of course, ruining Cora's day. She wanted things to fall apart, she wanted to take some kind of credit for early detection.

"It can't last, mark my word. Elaine can't take it. She's got her reputation to think of. How embarrassing it must be."

"Cora, you are wasting your time. Booker and Elaine love one another. He's a good man."

"He's a man, I'll grant you that. And they're all alike when it comes to you-know-what."

"Well, I hate to say it, Cora, but it seems to me you're projecting your own problems. I don't know if your Howard plays around, or ever has played around on you, but it sounds to me like you are a little insecure there, and so you go around thinking everybody else's husband does the same. I can assure you my Fritz never has looked at another woman. Sometimes I wish he would."

"Well, I never ... Really, Melissa, I don't know what's come over you. Has Aunt Tilly visited you? I am just concerned for a mutual friend, and you have had the bad manners to attack me in the most vicious way."

She stood up as if to go, but I knew her better than that. She would mill around, sizing up the state of my furniture, until I came around and apologized. And of course she would be back the next day, and I would feel bad for what I said about her

Howard. Howard did play around, I knew that, but still I was wrong for throwing it in her face. She was pretty shaky herself and she needed a friend. She didn't really have any, except myself and Elaine. Elaine was a rock for both of us, or an island toward which we swam, with our picnic basket of chicken bones.

When Elaine called later that day, I told her to be careful the next time Cora called, that she was in delicate shape and needed our friendship more than ever.

DEAR CUSTOMER

Before placing me on your shelf, please take me by the feet and give me a few hard shakes to help restore that 'just made' look. Thank you." I have been carrying these instructions around in my pocket for weeks, pulling them out at odd moments. I found them on the street and I don't know what they're for—perhaps a teddy bear's suicide note.

"Marrrrk," my wife yells at me, "Come here and tell me what the hell is coming out of the sink. It looks like some kind of puree of lizard."

This was to be our time, the rediscovery of one another as tender, loving beings, with a vague insinuation by our friends, who had been through the wars for twenty years, that we might even wake-up feeling nineteen years old, as when we first met, puppies in heat, blind heat. "I'll just drive down to the hardware store and see if they have some of the bacteria that eats things like this. Miracle stuff, thrives on backed-up puke."

Shirley from next door is scratching at the kitchen window, her words ricochet off the double thermal panes and scare several flickers into the overcast sky. Shirley is a perpetually depressed social worker who must smoke marijuana all day every day in order to put a dim sheen on her depression. But she seems to know something about this green stuff, or perhaps it is her own emergency whose import we fail to decipher.

"I'll just run down to Kentfield's and will be back with the stuff in a couple of minutes."

Florence looks at me, looks back at Shirley, who by now has collapsed out-of-view. The birds are back, completely oblivious to the nature of human suffering.

I've turned on the radio in the car. "...terrorism is the second largest industry ..." Well, of course, nowadays. What with the wall-units and the lawn slaves, what can you expect. The parasites found in sushi. In my day, romance was quite an adventure. Tourism, I see, he meant tourism.

A man's place is in the hardware store. No place like feeling like a Dad as in the hardware store. I take my time. Examine the merchandise, all of which I want, none of which I know how to use. When I describe my problem, today's specific problem, the son of the son of the owner looks at me as if I were a vile fetishist about whom he had had precise warnings. "Forget it," I say, pretending absentmindedness. "What I really need today are some bass plugs. You've got fishing lures, haven't you?" And I am overcome with that sense of randomness that I had left the house to avoid, hoping beyond hope to find some firm ground here at Kentfield's, the old family hardware store. "Is your father working today?" I ask genially, as though the kid had made a real fool of himself.

"He died three years ago."

Before placing on the shelf, a few hard shakes ...

Florence and Shirley are having tea on the front porch. I've never seen two more serene faces. They don't need me. The lizard has retreated. No sign of a mess anywhere. Their world is temporarily ordered. Recipes, children, the operations of mutual friends, fabrics, fall chores, local politics. They don't even look my way when I slam the side door.

They don't care that I have gargled dirt since this day began.

THE NEW TEACHER

There was a great deal of anticipation surrounding the arrival of the new junior high teacher, Olivia Gibbs, first, because she was new and from the East, which automatically lent her cultural superiority in the eyes of Mosly's self-effacing citizenry; and, secondly, because, from her resumé, it was clear Miss Gibbs had traveled widely and would bring a fresh perspective to the lives of those she touched. Her predecessor, Miss Evralena Sledge, had not had a new thought in fifty years when she keeled over during the Pledge of Allegiance one morning. Her students could barely suppress their desire to applaud as it was the quickest they had ever seen her move.

"I suppose she'll think we're a bunch of backwater simpletons and mental defectives from the dark ages," Emily McCormick was saying to the principal, Travis Skelton. "I hope we won't embarrass ourselves into scaring her away right off."

"Well, she must have seen something she liked in us or Mosly or both, because she's already bought herself a house." Mr. Skelton, being the principal of the Junior High, took some pride in the place and didn't plan on cringing before his newly hired teacher no matter where she'd gone to school or grown up. "She'll fit in in no time, you wait and see, Emily. Don't bother yourself so."

"I'm not bothered, Travis, I just want her to like Mosly. I think we should plan a little get-together to welcome her before classes start."

Mr. Skelton did like to savor every last minute of the summer, but he knew Emily was right. They should plan something.

"Why don't you take charge of it, Emily. Maybe ask Beth and Lorene if they will help you. See if Lorene will make one of her gooseberry pies."

Several of the teachers gathered at the party claimed they had seen Olivia Gibbs running errands around town during the summer, but none had actually spoken with her or met her face to face.

"She has such a sense of purpose," Lorene said. "I saw her at the bank, very dignified, but not off-putting. I watched her when she was taking out her mortgage loan. Old Billy Laminack was impressed."

"I can imagine," said Emily. "Of course, Billy Laminack was impressed when I introduced him to my cousin's goldfish, if you know what I mean."

Just then Olivia knocked on the screen door. "Hello everyone. Sorry if I'm late."

Emily took it upon herself to provide introductions. A dozen of the faculty had been rounded-up.

She really was attractive, tall, nicely dressed, and, best of all, she smiled comfortably, naturally, to each new colleague.

"I've had quite a week, let me tell you. I've been on the phone trying to get some honest answers from three of the agrichemical companies around here." Conversations stopped and heads turned toward Olivia. "You won't believe the level of emissions at Diamond Shamrock. I'm surprised half the town hasn't got bone and reproductive cancer. Well, you'll be glad to know I've called the EPA, called them ten times this week already, and they've promised some action. I'll settle for nothing short of closing down the plant. Until then, none of us are safe."

There was absolute silence in the room.

"Welcome to Mosly," Woody Weaver, the shop teacher, chimed.

"Oh, I'm sorry." Olivia recouped her sense of occasion. "What an impression I must be making on you. Please forgive me. It really is lovely to meet all of you. I'm very pleased to be here, really I am."

"My father and brother and all of my uncles work for Diamond Shamrock," Beth said.

Woody lit a cigarette and chuckled.

"Where is your new house located?" Travis inquired.

"It's at the end of Old Mill Trace," Olivia replied. "Very quiet and shady. I want to have you over as soon as I'm fully settled. I've made arrangements to have bottled water delivered every week. I had an analysis done of the local water, and you wouldn't believe it: benzene, clordane, heptador, endrin, dioxin, you name it. I'm definitely not going to cook with it, and only reluctantly will I bathe in it."

"I've never really given it a thought," Travis said. "I grew up here, never lived anywhere else, except when I was in the service. I guess we natives are immune or something. Have you tried the cheese dip, can I get you some?"

"No thanks, " Olivia said.

Woody Weaver pulled a small silver flask from his sports jacket and poured a dash of whiskey into his cup of punch. Miss Gibbs obviously amused him, and he was not above pursuing a little mischief. "Care for a dollop, Olivia?"

She knew a trap when she saw one, and surprised Woody by accepting the offer. "Why not?" But then she couldn't resist striking back. "Do you know, Mr. Weaver, that if I put one drop of pure nicotine on the tip of your tongue you would drop dead in less than three seconds?"

"Then I hope you won't do it," Woody said, and all those within ear-shot roared.

Emily was afraid things weren't going well. Olivia Gibbs was different from them, but surely there must be some common ground. They were, after all, all teachers. And, also, personally speaking, they were both women.

"You're not married are you, Olivia? I don't mean to . . ."

"Oh, that's all right. No, I am not married, never have been, never intend to. I like to make my personal choices, and from what I've observed, marriage is a constant compromise. I have a lot of friends . . ."

"I'll bet you do," Woody interjected.

Emily looked across the room at Beth, beseeching help, but Beth just laughed and shook her head.

"Is it true what I read that Mosly students have the lowest reading skills in the state?" Olivia asked Travis.

"Oh you read that, did you?" Travis replied, then turned and joined Woody in the corner.

Emily's welcoming party was turning into a tense and altogether unpleasant affair, and she only wished she had never had the idea at all. Perhaps they would have all gotten along together just fine if they had met their new colleague on the first day of classes. Maybe it would have taken years to discover their basic differences.

Olivia Gibbs stood there by herself in the middle of the room holding the drink from which she dared not sip. She felt that she had scored several important points already. Mosly was just a stepping-stone for her, she wanted to leave her mark, even on this putrid swamp, because that's how she did things.

HEDGES, BY SAM D'AMICO

One of the editors at *The Sunday Magazine* asked Sam D'Amico if he would write an article for them on the subject of Hedges. As co-owner of Barton's Nursery & Landscape, he was flattered and felt he must accept the challenge, even though he had never written anything more than a letter home to his parents from camp when he was a child.

"Hell," he told his wife Millie with his usual self-confidence, "I know everything there is to know on the subject, so what's the problem?" And that's when the problem began.

He told his partner, Ted, and all the other employees at the nursery, and they were suitably impressed. Sam even noticed a change in the way they addressed him or responded to his orders. And he liked this new respect. He dressed a little better than usual. Millie noticed this with interest and ribbed him gently about it. "You going to church?" she'd tease. He didn't mind because sometimes he needed her advice on coordinating outfits. He even took her with him when he decided to buy some new shirts and trousers. The new clothes were a little bolder, more colorful, than he was willing to wear previously.

The changes in his new style were introduced slowly at the nursery. Most of the workers didn't really notice. He carried himself with such quiet dignity now that they assumed it had always been so, that he was a man of distinction who occasionally dabbled in arts and letters. Only Ted saw the transformation, and he was glad for Sam, as he had been aware of Sam's recent depression. No big deal, Ted thought to himself, we all go through those periods when we're not sure of ourselves. when we question our worth. Now Sam's got something going for himself. Good for him.

"You know, Ted, I'm going to have to take a few days off to work on the article. Can you get by without me?"

"Hey, I understand, pal. No sweat. It's free advertising for the nursery. What could be better? Enjoy yourself."

They had covered for one another many times over the years. Ted's fishing trips, Sam's visits to his in-laws.

"You're a sport, Ted. Hey, wish me luck on this thing."

"You're the best, Sam, just remember that."

At home, Sam converted the guestroom into a study of sorts. He made a big desk out of a door he found in the cellar and a couple of saw-horses. He brought in one of the straight-backed chairs from the dining room. He placed a lamp on the desk and arranged a large yellow pad of paper and half-a-dozen freshly sharpened pencils next to the paper. He was rather proud of this improvised workroom.

"What do you think?" he asked Millie with a big smile on his face; what am I, the Ernest Hemingway of hedges, or what?"

"It's very nice, really. But wouldn't you be more comfortable in one of the stuffed chairs, I mean, for your back?"

HEDGES, BY SAM D'AMICO

"Hey, I'm not on vacation, baby. *This* is work. Your husband, the writer, star of *The Sunday Magazine,* on the fine science of hedges."

"Well, you better get to it. Ted was very nice to give you these three days." And with that remark she left the house to run some errands.

When she returned three hours later, she was surprised to find Sam sprawled on the couch watching an "All in the Family" re-run. He didn't even take his eyes off the set when she walked in front of him with two armloads of groceries. She set them on the kitchen counter and came back into the living room.

"Hey, what's with you, Señor Hemingway, all finished?"

He didn't like her joke. "It's too hot, I can't think straight."

"Well, did you get started at least?"

He made a face to indicate that she was annoying him. Finally he said, "How the hell do you know where to start? I mean, you know I know all this stuff, but how do I begin? 'Hi, my name's Sam D'Amico and here are a few tips on choosing your hedge, and here are a few pointers on planting your hedge.' That's not what those *Sunday Magazine* articles sound like."

She could see he was exasperated, but he had taken such pride in the invitation to write the article, she saw now she was going to have to build him up. That wasn't Sam's problem, usually.

"You're being silly. You can do it. I know you can. You're the expert, just think of it that way."

He was acting like a hurt child. Everything Sam did he did well, and this was the source of his whole identity. One year he even went out and bought a bunch of sex manuals just to be sure he was doing it like the experts said it should be done. He was insufferable. Millie counted the days until he would move on to some new project that didn't involve her.

"It's supposed to be 5,000 words, how can anyone *write* 5,000 words, for God's sake. How did I get into this? Millie, you've got to help me."

"I don't know the first thing about hedges. Now stop whining like a child. I've got an appointment at the hairdresser tomorrow morning so you'll have the house to yourself. In the afternoon I'm having lunch with Ruth okay? You'll have a nice quiet day to think and write and you'll see, it will come to you."

But Sam's day was not at all peaceful. First, he cleaned the basement cleaner than it had been in fifteen years. He threw out old paint cans and boxes. He made a trip to the dump and disposed of an ancient aquarium that had not seen a live fish in at least ten years. He threw away some wooden skis that he had bought at a tag sale years ago and never used. On his way back from the dump he stopped at the Tobacco Shop and bought himself a pack of cigarettes, his first since he was in the Navy.

In the study, he pulled the chair over to the window that looked out on Evelyn Turner's house. She was in the kitchen baking something. He had always wanted to see her in a swimsuit or less. But this was okay for now.

ABOVE THE RIVER

"Do you want to make love?" Wayne asked his wife, Evie.

"Here?" They were walking a trail on the bluff above the river. "But what if somebody comes along?"

"They won't. Besides, give them a little show. So what."

Evie looked down at the waterskiers below, and the families out boating on this sunny Sunday.

"Hey, it's our anniversary, we can do what we want, right?"

"What about bugs?" Evie looked at the grass around them. "Could be something lurking there."

"You always find excuses, you take the fun out of it, really you do, Evie. Why not try to be spontaneous like we were the first few years. Remember when we did it in the library stacks? Now that was dangerous."

"We were younger then, and dumber."

"We were healthy, we were in love." He paused and reached for her hand. "And, damn it, we're still healthy, and I, for one, am still in love."

"Remember when we did it in that boat? That was crazy." She smiled wistfully, as if all that were irretrievably lost.

"Come on. I'll put my jacket down. No bugs, you'll see. I will personally destroy any bug that even considers approaching your beautiful body. Come on."

A woodchuck stood up on its hind legs and looked at them.

"And what about that?" Evie pointed to the creature only a

few yards away. "Are we to corrupt that young woodchuck? It's probably only four months old, and you want to take the responsibility of performing a live sex show before an infant woodchuck. Really, Wayne, I thought you had better values than that."

She was funny, but Wayne was also getting annoyed. It was such a good idea, so harmless and well meant and, in her playful way, she was making sure it would not occur. So much for the anniversary.

"Let's just walk, okay?" Evie said, trying to make peace.

And they continued on their way along the path. The young woodchuck didn't duck for cover until they were four or five paces away from him.

Some storm clouds were moving in from the west, but they wouldn't be overhead for another hour. Two elderly women hikers were now behind them some distance down the path.

"See," Evie said, "We would have been caught in the act, definitely." She was right, but this didn't make Wayne feel one bit better.

"So?"

Evie didn't answer. Wayne was hurt. He looked down at the boaters and envied them. It was strange, not knowing them, imagining their lives. Maybe they were all married to axe-murderers and prostitutes. He cocked his arm and threw a stone as far as he could and moments later it made a small splash just at the edge of the water.

"Your mother called this morning to congratulate us. I forgot to tell you. When you were at the store. She says your father's not well, he's very depressed."

Wayne knew her ploy, to change the subject once and for all.

He played along, there was nothing else to do, either that or let an argument develop, and he was determined to keep the day free of any unpleasantness.

"He should have never retired, that's what it is," he said.

"You work forty-five years for the same company and get sick a month after you retire. It doesn't seem fair."

"Right."

Evie was sorry for bringing up the subject. Wayne worried about his father all the time now, though he seldom spoke to her about it. One reference a day was all he shared, but she knew.

"Let's head back, what do you say?"

They passed the two lady hikers on the path, and all four nodded politely without speaking.

"Very military," Wayne whispered to Evie, and she laughed in agreement. "Nazi Special Forces, Alpine Division."

"Oh stop it, now, you're being bad."

When they reached the car Evie sensed that Wayne was barely holding back tears. It had been a hard year for him—his sister's divorce, his father's illness, and she had been remote from him at times.

He opened the door for her and bowed, waving his hand grandly. "My princess," he said. She got in and leaned over to his side to unlock his door for him.

"That was a lovely walk," she said. "We'll have to come here more often. I bet it's lovely around dusk."

"Too dangerous," he said, "what with the Nazis and rodents and bugs. It's a miracle we're alive."

THE TORQUE-MASTER OF ADVANCED VIDEO

The new manager was an impish twenty-three year old named Arthur Tomten. His first day on the job he wore a button on his lapel which said *Wanna see my chainsaw?* and a tiny silver axe dangled from his left ear. He had five employees working for him, all older than himself, and all of whom had been working at the store for at least six months. It was only natural that they would initially resent his having been chosen from "outside" for the newly vacated position of manager. Still, there was not a great deal at stake since none of them were making much, if anything, above minimum wage, and the manager of the store only made a token amount more, and had to shoulder far more responsibility.

The five workers—Dave, Chris, Leslie, Don, and Richard—were eager to see what kind of boss Arthur Tomten would turn out to be. And Arthur himself was so young he too was eager to find out what kind of boss he would be. The second day on the job he lost the keys to the store—thanks to the hole in the pocket of his one decent pair of trousers, and the owner of the store was furious at him and demanded that all the locks on the store be changed immediately—at Arthur's personal expense, over $100 as it turned out. Arthur was humiliated and felt the instant loss of respect of his workers. It was not an auspicious beginning. The owner's name was Earl Smith. He had owned a shopping mall previously. He had nearly lost everything, but had recouped by investing in the newest hot trend, video rentals. He knew and cared nothing about movies, but was out to prove he was no fool. He bought any movie in sight, generally following the principal that the public wants garbage, more and more garbage, sex and violence and work-out videos, Rocky Fucks the Poor and Feels Good About It. So far it seemed to be working. But he had no humor, this owner. And when he visited the store on one of his surprise raids and found the employees loitering in the backroom joking with one another, he issued rigid orders, new rules, strict guidelines of behavior. Arthur would turn pink during these dressings-down, his frail pride withered, his anger well-corked. He felt like a bad child in military school, and he wondered what kind of a man he must be to tolerate such humiliation from a man he would never in a million years respect. Earl Smith embodied everything he detested in the older generations.

"Yes, Mr. Smith," he would reply, "I will see to it that all employees are kept busy every minute they are on payroll. You have my word there will be no more nonsense."

Smith would glare at the diminutive manager of his store. He would stare specifically at Arthur's button of the day and his violent earring.

"What the hell is that?" he'd asked, "You're a manager now, Tomten. You're representing my interests to the public." He couldn't bring himself to even mention the earring it infuriated him so. "Act like a man, can't you? I entrusted you with this responsibility and I expect you to make me proud of that trust I put in you. Do you get my message?" Now it was Smith who was red, and Arthur swallowed deeply to suppress the horrible laugh that was welling up in his bosom.

When Earl Smith left there was a collective sigh of relief and the workers went back to work pretty much as before. Their in-jokes were all that got them through the day. The work was, in fact, dreadfully boring. The customers were a peculiar lot of lonely, battered people. The garbage man from Belchertown who checked out "Seka's Fantasies" three times every week, the boat people with their obsession with Chuck Norris films, the college professors with their nervous fingering of risqué foreign imports. There weren't that many surprises or even pleasantries. Something about a VCR that says nowhere-to-go, no-one-to-speak-to, nothing-to-do, little-on-my-mind. And to stand behind a counter eight hours a day, five or six days a week, was a window on the world that needed constant cleaning.

Arthur's own obsession was with "splatter" films and biographies of serial killers. No one knew exactly why. He was sweet and polite and was refreshingly funny to his co-workers.

"That woman makes me want to throw up razor blades," he would say after a particularly unsavory customer had left the store. He didn't talk much about himself, but it was known that he lived with a girl, Angie, and that they were both from Shamokin, Pennsylvania. He loved both Angie and Shamokin. Shamokin had at least three major distinctions to its credit. One: Walter Winchell had said that the women of Shamokin were among the most beautiful in the world. Two: Groucho Marx had been given the key to Shamokin and had mentioned it on his TV program, "You Bet Your Life." And three: the noggin. The "noggin in a jar" is how Arthur always referred to it. It seems that sometime near the end of the last century a severed head had been found in the town park. No one knew what to do with it. An ad was placed in the newspaper so that anyone wanting to claim the head would know where to go. Days passed and no one claimed it. A week passed. It was beginning to decay and smell, so the temporary holders of the head had the good sense to embalm it. It was placed in a large jar of formaldehyde and years passed, decades, nearly a century. Arthur, as a young child and even later as a teenager, loved to visit the "noggin," as he had dubbed it. It sat on a shelf in the backroom of the town library. He took pride in his town for keeping it all these years. But then, one Christmas after Arthur had left home, the library burned to the ground and the noggin was no more. A sad loss.

As for the beautiful women of Shamokin, Arthur was particularly fond of recalling the lovely albino twins, Eunice and Eugenia Smitherman. They were considerably older, in fact, they were even older than Arthur's father, but thought of themselves as eternally sixteen. And, of course, they dressed as twins always, and would only consent to double-dates with brothers, which in the long run hurt their chances in a town as small as Shamokin. They, however, did not burn down and can still be seen occasionally in the malt shop or at their favorite dressmaker's.

Arthur's eyes actually twinkled when he told his tales of Shamokin. And Dave and Chris and the others laughed in appreciation and egged him on with questions. Arthur, essentially a private man, even in his youth, gradually revealed more of himself through these stories. His father was a prison guard who raised pigeons. His mother worked in an old age home. Arthur's girlfriend had been his high school sweetheart. They had lived together for almost five years, which meant, in effect, that Arthur had never had any other girlfriend. Angie was something of a mystery to the employees of Advanced Video. All they knew about her was that she too loved "splatter" films and that she had total power over Arthur. She made him move into another room in their apartment. Then she'd let him move back a little later. She even dated other men occasionally, and Arthur would be depressed for days.

Earl Smith was making a killing in his new business. He opened three more outlets and bought thousands of films. He'd make trips to distant warehouses and come back with a truckload of random trash. Growth, growth, and more growth. He had been rich eight or nine times before, he had lost count, but he always knew the way back out of bankruptcy. He could find the pulse, was how he liked to put it. Of course, everybody was always stealing from him, he knew this, but he figured it took more time to watch over them every second than it was worth in the long run. About Arthur Tomten he had mixed thoughts. The little guy certainly knew something about films, and he wasn't sure if this was an asset or a bother. Arthur was always trying to advise him on what the store needed, what kinds of films, and this partly annoyed Earl, though it was just possible that he needed someone like that, some film nut.

He didn't even remember the names of the others, just the managers. He'd blame all failures on them, that's why they got paid more than the others, the little shits.

"I want to know which films are not being checked out. I want you to go through all the records and give me a complete list of all films that aren't moving. Do you understand?"

"I understand," Arthur replied, filled with dread, knowing that this meant working nights for the next two weeks, knowing too that Angie would be fed up with him, that she would have ample opportunities to step out on him with her new interest, the Ph.D. political scientist creep she met the week before last.

He, Arthur, could not imagine a future without Angie. There had always been Angie. He and Angie, Shamokin, the noggin, the Smitherman twins. The Torque-Master, as he liked to call the owner of Advanced Video, was putting an end to all that, completely oblivious to the gravity of his situation.

"Listen up, Tomten. I've given you a chance here. I've trusted you. I could have promoted one of the others, but I didn't. You get this store moving in a big way, and there's something in it for you. You let me down and there won't be a second chance. Understand? Two of the other stores are already doing greater volume. You're slipping. Now you run a tight ship here or else. Do you follow me?"

"I follow you. I'll have the list for you next week at the managers' meeting."

"That's more like it," Smith snarled. He was like some kind of despicable football coach, never satisfied, always insulting, with no notion of human dignity. And Arthur despised himself for not telling him to his face. What kind of sniveling chattel was he becoming? In Shamokin he and Angie had always thought they didn't need anyone else, they had this unspoken contract with one another that nothing could tarnish their private world as long as they remained strong and true to one another. They knew when the world was false, they knew what it was they would do and what was beneath them. Now, he had to earn a living somehow, but the harder he worked, the closer he was to losing all that he was working for. Angie was changing. She was not amused by their old habits, watching horror films, listening to bizarre music, putting down most everyone around them. She wanted to go back to school and finish her degree. She even talked of moving to New York.

"Look at you," she said to him one night, "in your little Salvation Army pin-striped suit and bow tie." (Her emphasis on the word "little" was "a hat pin in his eye" he told Leslie and Don at the store.) "If you're going to be a capitalist, then do yourself a favor and don't be such a wimpy, pitiful one. Your little protest earrings are really a big statement. You're going to change the world with amusing buttons, I suppose?"

Arthur worked late every night now, he had to, he had no choice. The shelves of the store were crammed with films nobody cared about, How to Make Your Head Explode films, films about insect life in Asia, How to Raise a Baby Underwater, Travelogues of Cemeteries, How to Sculpt Used Tires, How I Married a Dead Junkie and Found Happiness. There was even a homemade video of a seventeen year old boy's suicide made by his older brother.

THE TORQUE-MASTER OF ADVANCED VIDEO

Arthur hadn't even known about this one. He read the jacket-copy on the box and smiled. He shoved the paperwork to one side of the office desk, then pushed the cassette into the VCR and leaned back. Surely he deserved a break after so many pages of figures. But it was Angie he was thinking of the whole time, how they had first gotten together. It always had been a kind of suicide pact, he realized now, and now that he was really dying, she was breaking the pact. It wasn't funny one bit. What had they been laughing at all this time. It wasn't one bit funny.

THE EXAMINATION

Dr. Shroeder, at the age of thirty-four, had every reason to be pleased with himself. The spacious new house with its solar heating system came complete with a little apartment in back for his mother. And his new black BMW made him feel sportier than he actually was, and he liked this, and told no one that he had to sit on a pillow to be able to see over the steering wheel. With his practice growing day by day, the six-figure income helped compensate for his premature baldness and the curse of his diminutive height. He was tall of mind, he liked to say. His mother had taught him to say that when he was teased in high school.

At the clinic he demanded complete respect from his nurses. They brought him coffee between patients and they removed the Styrofoam cups from his desk each morning before he arrived. They, Susan and Patty, often asked one another why it was not possible for the great doctor to simply dispose of the cups in his wastebasket himself. But it was a small matter, and they knew he was a stickler for detail. Everything had to be just the way he wanted it or he would have one of his little tantrums. He would not walk across the room for a tongue depressor. It had to be right by his left hand as he was examining the patient.

When a female patient required a vaginal examination, one of the nurses was always present, and Dr. Shroeder's behavior was as cool and thoroughly professional as could be, betraying nothing but medical satisfaction that he could remedy the problem. And when the patients were young and beautiful and shapely, Patty or Susan watched the doctor's every expression in hope of detecting some interest or stimulation, but, alas, his little round stone face was a perfect blank.

One spring morning, on his way to the clinic, listening to classical music on his tape-deck, Dr. Shroeder accidentally drove over a pair of birds copulating in the middle of the road. His heart jumped and he looked quickly in the rear-view mirror. Sure enough, they were thrashing wretchedly, and he couldn't help but wish another car would come along in a moment and finish them off. While making love! Perpetuating their species! And he, a doctor! He quickly put them out of his mind and looked at his clipboard on the seat beside him. Ah, Mrs. Ramstetter.

Mrs. Ramstetter was truly statuesque, she towered above him like a Scandinavian goddess. She was seated in the waiting room reading an old issue of *Natural History*. She had called the day before and Dr. Shroeder was able to fit her in this morning.

"The doctor will see you now," Patty told Mrs. Ramstetter.

Mrs. Ramstetter sat in the examination room for several minutes before the doctor entered. She had been coming to Dr. Shroeder for almost two years now and they had struck up some small rapport. She was a healthy, vigorous woman, occasionally plagued by small complaints. This time it was the little finger on her right hand. It had been stiff and sore and slightly swollen for more than a month and she wondered if she might not have some rheumatoid arthritis in it.

The doctor held her hand and bent the joints of her little finger back and forth with great concentration. She felt just a little silly taking up his time for a complaint so small, but his rapt attention dissuaded her embarrassment. Indeed, she began to wonder if that stiff little finger might not bode something more serious, or why else would the doctor have then asked her to disrobe and put on one of his robes.

Dr. Shroeder left the room while she stepped out of her skirt and blouse. Mrs. Ramstetter then sat on the edge of the examination table and thought to herself how the little finger might express some larger malady. Normally, she had confidence in medical science.

When Dr. Shroeder returned, he asked Mrs. Ramstetter to open her robe so that he could examine her breasts. She complied automatically. There was something vaguely comical about his tiny hands exploring her large, full breasts. He had to reach up to them and had an underside view of them. Nonetheless, he seemed to savor the work, taking his time, doing the most thorough examination possible, if that is what it should properly be called, Mrs. Ramstetter thought to herself. Then she began to feel the sweat on his little palms, and she looked down at his bald pate and saw glistening beads of sweat there also.

Mrs. Ramstetter felt completely violated by this little runt of a man, and still she could not bring herself to speak. Dr. Shroeder told her she could get dressed now and again he left the room.

When he returned, he seemed shaken and stared down at his clipboard as he attempted to talk with her. "It appears you have the beginnings of a little rheumatoid arthritis. It's nothing serious and will most likely go into remission. It might come back in five or ten years, but I don't believe, in your case, it will ever become serious."

Mrs. Ramstetter considered her options: if she told him just what she thought of his little fun with her, what did she have to gain? She finally decided that she had more to lose and said nothing but "Thank you, doctor, for seeing me on such short notice."

That night, and for the next several nights, Stanley Shroeder dreamed of those breasts, his hands stretching to encompass as much of their girth as possible, and then in circling motion he massaged them. But then, each time he woke with a start when they became those two unsuspecting birds, black and screeching in their death dance.

"Stanley," his mother called through the wall that separated them, "Are you all right, darling?"

OUR COUNTRY COUSINS

Once a year Nikki and I pile in the car for the cross-country journey to visit our families. We usually go in the summer, hot as blazes, and, once there, there are a series of picnics held by lakes. The nephews and nieces shoot up six inches a year until they land in jail or go away to college. In our families, they never go far. Nikki and I are the only ones to have settled out of state; and we are therefore treated differently. Our presence seems to excite most of the family, as though our stories were of another civilization. We try not to disappoint them, and we are delighted with their accents. Ours come back to us almost immediately. But no one in either family has visited us where we live. We accepted this without much thought, until we got the call from Nikki's aunt and uncle, Lloyd and Joan. They wanted to come for a week in June. We had no choice in the matter, and instantly started to panic.

They wouldn't know what to make of any of our friends, and we probably didn't have any interests in common, once you stripped away the family thing.

"Let's not worry about it until they get here," Nikki advised. "I've known them all my life. And they love us both, you know that, Charles. They'd do anything for you."

"But it's different. When we're there, we're different people.

We both try to blend in. Here, I don't know, it makes me nervous. What will we do to kill time? Lloyd doesn't have any interests, I mean, ones that travel well."

"We'll take long drives."

I had forgotten just how loud Lloyd could be until he stepped out of his car in our driveway. "Not bad, Charlie, old boy! Not bad at all! Glad to see somebody in the clan is making it."

It was good to see them, but already I was aware of our neighbors staring our way, probably amused, possibly annoyed at Lloyd's decibel crashing of the property-line.

"By George, so this is where you've hidden our little Nikki all these years."

We spirited them inside as quickly as we could. Joan glanced around at the paintings on the walls. Nikki and I looked at one another and realized our mistake. Most of the paintings should have been stored for the duration of this visit. The big nude study by our friend Noel Clemmins identified us as Communist subversives right away. Joan tried not to look at it, but it kept sneaking its way back into her peripheral vision. Obviously I have turned her little niece Nikki into a swinger and pervert of the worst sort.

Joan was very nearly speechless at the sight of our furniture, as well. We were touted by Nikki's mother as grand successes of some kind. Nikki's mother had this competition with her sisters, and we were obviously displayed in our absence as the ones who traveled regularly in Europe, who mixed with a few famous politicians. There wasn't a great deal of truth to the picture she painted, but we gave her ammunition over the phone occasionally that could be used to intimidate her sisters. Now Joan was quietly gloating at the disheveled appearance of our home, the paintings in poor taste, the tear in the fake oriental carpet. She could hardly wait to report back the seamy truth.

"Lloyd, can I get you a beer?" I asked to break the tension. I knew Joan didn't drink, but I thought, away from the rest of the family, I might get Lloyd to loosen up.

He glanced at Joan sheepishly. "A brew sounds good."

"Just one." Joan informed him. "Well, Nikki, you look like you've lost weight since we saw you last summer. You haven't been sick or anything have you?"

"Please, sit down, have a chair," Nikki said. "No, I've been well. I always lose a couple of pounds in the summer. We've been swimming everyday. And we eat a lot lighter in the summers."

"Tofutti," Lloyd said.

"What was that, Uncle Lloyd?"

"Tofutti. Do you eat that new stuff, tofutti?"

"No," Nikki laughed, "we're not into fads. What's this tofutti, I've never heard of it."

"You see, you don't know everything. Tofutti, some kind of health food, an ice cream substitute, and you've never heard of it. You see, Joan, they don't know everything."

I gave Lloyd his beer and Joan gave me one of her looks. She hated Noel's painting. It was against everything she had ever stood for her whole life. Nudes in the living room, really.

OUR COUNTRY COUSINS

We took them out to dinner that first night to an old, elegant country inn. It went well enough, except for the wine. They both thought we were affected and unnatural for not drinking coffee with our meal. But we had decided that we should be ourselves and stop apologizing for who we were. We asked them a lot of questions about their three kids, all grown now, and we talked about Nikki's parents and my parents. In fact, we talked about everything but ourselves. And they never asked us a single question about our lives. They had driven a long way to see us and, as far as they were concerned, they had seen enough. The trouble was that they had said they were staying a week.

Lloyd looked around the Inn and summed it up: "This looks like the kind of place you could make one of those horror films." We didn't respond so he amplified his meaning. "You know, an axe murderer, blood flowing down the staircases, I can just see it."

"It's very historic," Nikki replied. "A lot of famous men have slept here."

"Yeah, I bet. Like Jack the Ripper." He roared at his own joke, and the maitre d' looked our way with displeasure.

"Lloyd," Joan said, "you're embarrassing Charles and Nikki. You forget you're not at home. People act differently here."

"Are you asking me to change at my age? 'Cause if you are, darlin', I got some real bad news for you."

"Uncle Lloyd," Nikki said, "Princess Grace of Monaco had lunch here a few years ago."

"And look where it got *her*," he said, choking at his own wit. "Like I said, a good horror picture could be made right here.

Don't get me wrong, I like some of them pictures, too. Hell, I'd go see it."

"Watch your language, Lloyd." Joan said.

We were relieved to get back to the house. Lloyd and Joan were in bed by 9:30. Neither Nikki nor I could fall asleep that early. We talked in hushed voices for several hours, desperate for a plan.

When we got up the following morning at seven it was obvious that our guests had been awake for some time. They'd drunk one pot of coffee and Lloyd was complaining in his familiar jokey way about what a man had to do to get breakfast around this place.

"It's a good thing you aren't a farmer's wife, Nikki, do you know that, little darlin'? Now what about some pancakes? You do know how to make pancakes, don't you?"

"Of course I know, Uncle Lloyd, you just hold your britches on, and I'll start breakfast in a few minutes."

Joan offered to help in the kitchen, and Nikki accepted the offer, partly, I think, to give me a chance to wake up without her watchful eyes measuring my every scratch and wrinkle. I still couldn't get over how different it was having them in our own house. They were like complete strangers to us, except that we knew their thoughts. Back home I could tease and joke with both of them, and they liked it. Here, I was afraid to josh with them in the same way.

"What do you want to see today, Lloyd? There's a lot of old towns around here that might interest you. The birthplaces of six presidents are within a couple hours driving distance. We've got your Millard Filmore, your Calvin Coolidge."

"Weak ones."

"What's that?"

"I said, you grow weak presidents in this part of the country. Hell, we didn't drive all the way out here to visit Millard Filmore's birthplace when we got Truman and Eisenhower practically next door at home."

"Well," I said, "we'll let the ladies decide."

"I know what Joan wants to do. She already told me this morning when you two were sleeping-in. She wants souvenirs, you know, to prove to her girlfriends back home that she was actually here. Souvenirs are the only way to make believers of them. Joan is practically obsessed with getting souvenirs on this trip. She already said she won't be back in this lifetime, so I hope you know where they've got the best ones."

"Well," I said, "Living here as we do, I haven't given the subject a whole lot of thought, but I'm sure we'll come up with something."

Lloyd gave me a look at those words, and I revised myself in a hurry: "I don't mean just something; we'll definitely find the best place."

And, after breakfast, we began our search for the best souvenirs in the area. We must have driven two-hundred miles in our effort to satisfy Joan's quest. We stopped at fifteen or so such shops, and they all contained pretty much the same crap you would find in any part of the country. But this didn't lessen Joan's passion. She bought three or four items in each shop. She was consumed with concentration, and talked out-loud to herself as she browsed from table to table: "Hilary would just love this, Suzanne would get a kick out of this, wouldn't she, Lloyd? Bill and Yvonne love little things like this." It caught me off guard how suddenly she delighted in risqué humor. Some of the tawdry junk even embarrassed me. Nikki and I mostly just stood there, pretending to examine racks of postcards. Twenty minutes to a shop, and then we'd barrel on down the highway a few miles until another such shop announced itself. We spent the entire day doing this, and both Lloyd and Joan seemed entirely satisfied. When Judgment Day comes, this day should not be held against me, as I did not really exist. Joan must have spent several hundred dollars on bric-a-brac, little outhouses, tomahawks, ashtrays, giant pens and stuff. The trunk was brim-full of her souvenirs, souvenirs from a place she hadn't even seen. She had the glazed look of one who had waited a lifetime to play her trump card, and now that she had played it successfully, there was nowhere left to go. Nikki and I didn't exist, and Lloyd was happy for her. Their trip was, in effect, over. She would count and recount her loot, imagining the responses she would get from Hilary, Suzanne and Yvonne.

"Maybe we could take them over to the Rudman's potluck tomorrow night," I said to Nikki in bed that evening. "They're nice people, they wouldn't mind."

"Oh, Charles, I don't know how we're going to last five more days. They just don't seem to have any curiosity about anything here."

"One day at a time, Nikki. We'll make it. I may be crazy by the time they go, but we'll make it somehow. It doesn't seem natural that we wouldn't introduce them to some of our friends. They'll go back home thinking we don't have any."

"Right now I'm not sure I care what they say about us, really. I always liked them so much. I can hardly believe I lived with them one whole summer. Their house was like a second home to me, and now I don't know what to talk about with them."

Elliott and Becca Rudman's potluck supper was no different than any of a dozen such gatherings we had attended at their house, the same eighteen or twenty people, the same range of dishes—all good, if a trifle out-of-the-ordinary. Lloyd and Joan clung to our sides as though they had been warned about this kind of crowd, as though rare forms of venereal diseases were transmitted by sneezes and handshakes at gatherings such as this one. Elliott Rudman tried to be the polite host, asking them where they lived and all the basics, but Lloyd was defensive and edgy and Elliott finally drifted away. I couldn't blame him. I wanted nothing more than to hide, but I knew Nikki would kill me if I abandoned her. Joan was positively ogling.

"Are these people your friends?" she asked Nikki in a tone of withering scorn.

"Some of them. Others I hardly know. They're perfectly nice people, Aunt Joan, really. That man over there is an anthropologist, and that woman there, her father is a leading heart surgeon."

"I think they dress funny. Fifty year old women dressed like teenagers. Are they poor or what's the problem?"

"Oh, no. Most of them are professional people. I guess it's just the style here."

"You call that style? I call it lack of style. Are they all atheists, too, I suppose?"

"Aunt Joan, as I told you, they're very nice people. I don't pry into other people's religious views."

"Humph," was all Joan could say to that.

"Let's get something to eat, what do you say, Lloyd? Are you hungry Joan? The food's on the table out on the deck. Come on while the picking's still good."

"This ought to be good," Lloyd said sarcastically. "This is the skinniest bunch of so-called adults I've seen since The Depression."

Everybody but Joan and Lloyd seemed very happy with the variety of dishes. They stood around on the deck eating off paper plates and complimenting one another on what they had prepared. This was a seasoned bunch of potluckers and they gave thought to the dishes they had brought. When it came our turn to help ourselves, Lloyd and Joan looked utterly depressed and made no motions toward any of the offerings.

"What's that?" Lloyd asked with obvious displeasure. People were beginning to watch us and listen to the rude comments our guests were making.

"Tabouli," Nikki answered, in an upbeat voice. "Try some, Uncle Lloyd. It's very healthy."

"I'm already healthy," he said. "What I am now is hungry."

"Why don't you just tell us what all this is," Joan said, "and we'll decide what's eatable, okay?"

"Well," Nikki said, looking around at the other guests looking at us, "this is spanakopita, a Greek spinach pastry."

"A spinach pastry? Whatever happened to just plain old cream puffs."

"And this is ratatouille, that's a Mediterranean vegetable stew."

"Where in the hell are we, anyway? Don't you have hams in this part of the country?"

"Now, Lloyd," Joan said, "don't be rude."

"And, let's see, this must be falafel, that's an Israeli chickpea croquette, very spicy and good. I bet you'd like that, Joan."

"I've sort of lost my appetite, if you know what I mean. Where's that thing you brought, Nikki? You made a strawberry shortcake, didn't you?"

"Yeah, I'd eat some of that," Lloyd said. "At least we can eat dessert now and get a burger when we leave."

"Actually, it's a strawberry tort . . ."

"Tort, short, I don't give a damn. At least it came from America, didn't it?"

People were trying not to laugh at us. It was so obvious that both Nikki and I were miserable, trying to accommodate some distant relatives we barely knew.

We found Nikki's tort and Lloyd and Joan took large slices for themselves.

"If you ask me," Joan said too loudly, "Nikki made the best dish of everybody."

Nikki's face turned red, and we exchanged looks: this simply was not working, a bad idea. Silently, we agreed to leave as soon as Lloyd and Joan finished their dessert. The other guests made no attempt to talk with us now. Even Elliott and Becca gave us wide berth when they crossed the deck to join another group.

When Joan had cleaned her plate she told Nikki she had to go to the bathroom. Nikki told her where she could find it, but then Joan turned around after she had stood up and said to Nikki, loud enough for all to hear, "Watch my purse."

When we woke the next morning there was a note left for us on the kitchen counter: THANKS FOR A WONDERFUL TIME, Love, Uncle Lloyd and Aunt Joan.

Trying to make Nikki feel better, I said: "I think they did have a good time. Joan got her souvenirs, and Lloyd will be telling stories about the Rudman's potluck supper for years to come. Don't feel bad. You'll see, next summer they'll have a thousand jokes at the picnic. And we'll be teasing them. You'll see, Nikki. That was the trip of their lives."

EATING OUT OF MOUSETRAPS

I had become dependent on that one glass of wine every night to relax me," Valerie was saying. "I couldn't sleep without it. I rarely if ever had a second glass, but still it was a dependence, and that's when I decided I had a problem." Valerie sipped at her juice with a newfound moral authority that made her feel very good about herself. The other women at the table stared incredulously at her at first, and then shifted their eyes back to their drinks with sinking hearts. It was supposed to be a carefree evening, no men allowed. Now they sat in silence until Valerie regained her momentum.

"And that's when I discovered AA. It is the most wonderful group of people I've ever met. Strangers come right up to you and say, 'Hi, my name is Jack and I'm an alcoholic.' 'Nice to meet you,' I say, 'My name is Valerie and I'm an alcoholic.' You're accepted immediately; everyone's so honest and personal. And you wouldn't believe the variety of people, doctors, policemen, housewives, professors, artists, salesmen."

The women at the table exchanged guarded looks with one another, not because they couldn't believe that doctors and policemen could be alcoholics, but, well, one glass of wine?

Valerie continued: "You don't have to tell your story to the group right away, but I wanted to, I wanted to get started on my recovery—though once an alcoholic always an alcoholic, you know. So I stood up and said, 'Hello, my name is Valerie and I'm an alcoholic. I drink every night etc. etc.,' and they applauded me and later that night they told me who my partner would be, the person I could call any time of night or day if I was tempted to take a drink."

"The doctor, I hope," Barbara said, attempting to lighten the mood.

"Well, no, I'm sorry to say I wasn't that lucky. My partner, well, I can't tell you her name. But I will tell you that it's a woman and, boy, let me tell you, she's one of the fattest, ugliest old sows you've ever set your eyes on. She worked at the mill for thirty years in Turner's Falls, says she kept a pint of vodka in her purse, spiked Coke all day long, then drank herself into oblivion each night when she got home to her one room apartment. She had no living relatives that she knew of since her mother died when she was sixteen, and of course she was always so fat no one wanted to marry her."

"I'd drink, too," said Barbara.

"Well, yeah. But think of my bad luck in getting stuck with such a depressing partner. I mean, I thought it was going to be fun, you know." Bobbie reached for her glass of wine and took a deep draught. The others glanced around and did the same.

"Well," Valerie continued, "What do you think happened when I got home the first night?"

"Fatso calls," quipped Barbara. There was laughter now no longer suppressed.

"Right. And let me tell you, I've never had such a *depressing* phone call in my life. At midnight, no less. And drunk! I mean, she wasn't just sipping, she was blasted out of her gourd! Nearly incoherent, I couldn't understand half of what she said. Rambling on about her job and her dead mother, and at some point I think she said, 'You don't need to dry out, you stupid little pigeon, you need to get soaked.' I don't know if those were her exact words because she was hacking and slurring so badly through the whole call. But can you imagine, my first night home from AA and I get an obscene phone call from my partner?"

Bobbie moved around the table filling everyone's glass but Valerie's, who had finished her juice. Marge, who hadn't spoken a word in an hour, said, "What did you think you were getting into, the D.A.R.?" More laughter. Valerie looked wounded.

"That wasn't very nice," she said.

"So what did you do, did you go back to the meeting the next night?" Barbara asked, attempting to take Valerie's mind off her tiny wound.

"Oh, yes, I went back, but I was a little scared this time. Of course I was hoping, you know, my partner wouldn't be there."

"And was she?"

"Yes, I'm afraid she was. She acted as if nothing had happened, just as polite as the first time I had met her, you know. 'My name's so-and-so and I'm an alcoholic.' Just the same."

"Did she apologize?"

"No, she never mentioned the call. The meeting went well, everybody cheerful and positive, telling their stories and thanking god and promising to be there for their partners if tempted to take a drink."

EATING OUT OF MOUSETRAPS

Barbara and Bobbie and Marge were losing interest in Valerie's self-absorption and just wanted to have a few laughs before it was time to go home. Valerie had succeeded as she often had in the past in thrusting herself and her problems to the forefront of an evening that was intended for fun, gossip and laughs. In truth, this would probably be the last time she was invited to join them for their special women's night at one of their homes. They just wouldn't tell her the next time they decided to get together.

"You can't believe what happened when I got home that night," she started up again.

"Oh, yes we can," said Bobbie, rather rudely.

"You can?"

"Sure. Fatty called again, drunk as a pig, and insulted the hell out of you. Right?"

"Yeah, that's right. But don't you think that's incredible? I mean, I went there for help and what did I get but a drunk, obscene phone caller. That isn't fair, is it? What do you think I should have done? Shouldn't I have reported her to somebody, the police or somebody?"

"She's your partner," Marge offered, "I thought you were supposed to help her."

"But how can I help someone like that, I mean, she's disgusting. That woman has real problems ..."

"Exactly," Barbara said. "That's exactly the point."

"I don't get it, I don't get it at all," Valerie said, looking depressed and deeply puzzled. "It looked like it was going to be such fun. I thought we were all going to be such good friends."

"Maybe you should try some EST training. Those people go to bed early and never call one another."

"Are you guys making fun of me? If you are, I think that's pretty cruel, I really do."

"Valerie, honey, why don't you get an unlisted number. Or better yet, have a glass of wine and try to forget your partner ever existed. I don't think you are going to help each other very much."

Valerie was staring at her wound again. She had been so proud of herself for admitting that she was an alcoholic, and now nobody seemed to be taking her seriously. She really hated the fat woman in Turner's Falls for taking all the fun out of it. She hoped the miserable sow would drink herself to death soon. Then she could go back to the meeting and surely this time she would get assigned a really attractive partner and they could talk about their problems without getting so rude about it.

ALMOST A MAN

Franklin Quigly Denton III arrived at his personal sense of superiority early in life. His father, Franklin Quigly Denton II, was an unhappy lawyer in a small milltown and told his son right away that most people were horses' asses and that was that. Franklin III liked his name immensely, and in that small milltown it immediately set him off from the rabble. He liked that and always walked the few respectable streets of the town with his chin up and a spring in his gait. It was quite a laughable sight to the old folks rocking on their porches in the summer. Such a little button-nosed arrogance in one so small. And he would never condescend to play with the children of the millworkers. And there were no other lawyers in town. Which left Franklin III all to himself to parade the neighborhoods as if he were destined for a great mission in this life.

Of course his mother had no equals either, and occupied a class all her own, which meant that she couldn't really join any clubs without *slippage*. She would lunch alone or with her son at the hotel restaurant and smile distantly across the room at anyone she suspected of staring or stealing looks. Mr. Denton would not have allowed her to associate with riff-raff, if she was so inclined, but of course she wasn't.

Franklin III was given piano lessons from the age of four, and his mother soon spoke of his becoming a concert pianist. She groomed him for the great stages of Europe: Franklin Quigly Denton III. She even imagined herself accompanying him on some of the grander tours, audiences with the great Kings and Queens . . . If she read the newspapers, of course, she would have known that most of them had long since lost their heads or were, at least, chased into anonymous exile, but nonetheless this was how she imagined the future for little Franklin and herself. The other flaw in this thinking was that little Franklin was not very good at playing the piano; he detested his teacher and rarely practiced. His teacher, a Miss Murphy, had dirt under her fingernails and sometimes smelled like a fish. Franklin, against his mother's orders, sometimes held his nose when he sat beside Miss Murphy on the piano bench. After nine months of tolerating this insult, she finally was forced to quit even though it meant taking in more laundry and ironing.

Another teacher was found, and Mrs. Denton went right on dreaming about Milan and Paris and Berlin. She had actually gone so far as to survey her closets and plan her wardrobe. She did not share her thoughts with Mr. Denton because she knew he did not approve of his only son becoming a concert pianist. Slippage for the family name. A lawyer was a manly and powerful thing to be, though he despised Law itself. The notion of equality before the law was odious to him. A bunch of horses' asses.

The piano lessons continued for twelve years. More than twenty teachers came and went. Franklin III mocked the way they dressed and the way they spoke. And, of course, his progress was painfully slow; and in the end even Mrs. Denton had difficulty sustaining her hopes that his name would ever grace any marquee grander than the local V.F.W.'s. However, it should be stated that this failure in no way distracted from the other, quite general conviction that Franklin III was cut of the finest timber, that his destiny was still to rule, to lead, to star in life's pageant.

Franklin did not play sports as a student in high school because he did not like to sweat, but also because he could not imagine showering with the coarse ruffians who tended to be on the teams. Instead, he preferred to practice putting by himself in his backyard. His father had always told him that putting was terribly important for a man to do well.

Franklin had always taken it for granted that he would be accepted at any college he should choose. His father had as much as told him so. His father's alma mater, Caldicott, for instance, would have to accept him because of the donations Mr. Denton made each year. And beyond that, the President of the college, Bernard Smythe, was a classmate of Mr. Denton. "There's loyalty there, son. That's something you can count on in this world, loyalty of the old school tie. Barney can be counted on. I've done him a favor or two in my time."

"But, Father, I've been thinking of applying to Chestnut Hill."

"Dentons have gone to Caldicott for three generations. It's a fine school. But if you prefer to break with tradition, I'll see what I can do."

Franklin said no more and secretly sent in his application to Chestnut Hill. Four weeks later he was stunned when the letter arrived informing him that his grades and test scores were not high enough for admission. He was only happy that he had not told anyone of his application to Chestnut Hill. He knew he would have the burden of carrying this rejection within him the rest of his life—that, in a way, he would always be lying now. Chin up!

It came as something of a shock when it was announced that he had been chosen class valedictorian, because he didn't really know most of his classmates. It was his name they had chosen, not him. But still it pleased him, and Mr. and Mrs. Denton, while proud, presumed it as a matter of course. Of course, Franklin III was the only obvious choice to say farewell and sum up, to look into the future.

At the graduation ceremony, Mr. and Mrs. Denton had front row seats reserved for themselves, and in their minds it was Franklin III's graduation and no one else's. What could those scruffy children possibly do but work in the mill? When it was Franklin's time to deliver his speech, Mr. and Mrs. Denton sat erect and gazed up at the podium as if final proof of their superiority were about to be delivered with undeniable finality. He was greeted with faint but polite applause. He began his speech with a kind of humorless pomp, in much the same tone his father employed when he was asked to speak on certain occasions.

He said: "A man must stand on his principles, or else he risks joining the common masses, the pagan elements at the bottom of the social ladder who wallow in drink and lechery, and who are a burden to the state." Mr. Denton swelled with pride at his son's high-mindedness. But Mrs. Denton shivered and realized that this young man, her son, already sounded like an old man. He made no references to his classmates or to his experiences at school. In many ways it was an odd speech, and parents in the audience shifted in their chairs and coughed a lot, and his classmates were throwing airplanes at one another, completely oblivious to Franklin's lofty oratory except for a certain amount of uncontrollable tittering. "I've always said you have to decide between action and contemplation." It was clear to those who were still listening that Franklin Quigly Denton III had chosen contemplation. And that made Mrs. Denton reflect on the innumerable hours of solitary putting she had observed Franklin practicing, and now she realized that in fact he was contemplating something. What, she thought to herself, what do you suppose he was contemplating? It was a rich thought for her to contemplate now. There was next to no applause as Franklin rather too grandly completed his valedictory address and took his place in the row of chairs at the front of the stage. "Way to go, Three!" someone shouted. Mr. Denton looked around, displeased at the disrespect.

Mrs. Denton was vaguely troubled after Franklin's speech and graduation. She couldn't quite put her finger on it, but it had something to do with young Franklin's insistence on the primary importance of a man's principles. Mr. Denton, she knew, was nothing if not a man of principles, but she also knew that deep down he didn't really believe in anything. And she feared that her son ... oh well, he was still such a young man, just starting out on his adventure.

Franklin wrote home every week from Caldicott, detailing his every activity. He had joined his father's old fraternity, which made Mr. Denton happier than his wife had ever seen him.

"That's my boy," he said, pacing the living room. "He's going to turn out all right, you'll see, you'll see. He had me worried there for a while. Those damned piano lessons were a waste of time, you wouldn't listen to me. I know what's best for my son. He's going to be all right. Law, that's the ticket. Or a broker, yes, that would be all right. Wall Street. You'll see, he's going to be just fine."

And when in his second semester he wrote saying that he had declared himself to be a Philosophy major, Mr. Denton took it right in stride. "Not to worry," he told Mrs. Denton, "State Department. Diplomacy. Quite common. Philosophy. Yes, I believe old Digges, Richard Digges, studied Philosophy at Caldicott, and look where he is. New Zealand. Ambassador. Yes, Philosophy is not a bad place to start." Mrs. Denton contemplated that awhile and decided that it probably was a very sensible place to start, though she wasn't exactly sure she knew what it was, Philosophy.

Of course, Mr. Denton thought privately that it didn't much matter what a good man studied *per se*. It was your fraternity brothers, those early contacts, that provided the ladder to success and the safety net should a good man ever stumble along the way. Franklin had already latched onto that ladder and there was no rocking him off now. So he didn't worry one jot when Franklin wrote home in his fourth semester to inform them that he had changed his major to English. "English," Mr. Denton said to his wife, "is a fine major. Good start for either a lawyer or a diplomat."

And when he wrote again six months later to tell them of his change to Art History, all Mr. Denton had to say on the subject was that his son was a regular Renaissance man. Yes, a Renaissance man, he like those words. Ambassador to France.

When they visited him on Parents' Day, Franklin ordered one very dry Martini at dinner, "Straight up, Boodles Gin. You do have Boodles, don't you?" And luckily they did. He's already taking a stand, Mr. Denton thought to himself. Several students passed their table and slapped young Franklin on the back. "What say, Quigly?" Mrs. Denton did not like that at all. Were they mocking her son? She supposed they were. Or just youthful affection. Franklin didn't seem to mind or notice. He seemed very pleased with himself, as he always had, but more so now. Caldicott had finally provided him with some worthy peers and, while there never was any question that things would "turn out" for Franklin, both Mr. and Mrs. Denton now felt he was in the home stretch, that he was a certain winner.

"I have some rather good news for you now," Franklin announced. "I have a woman with whom I am thinking of hooking-up. She's a Trowbridge."

"John Trowbridge?" inquired Mr. Denton. "A fine man. Old money. I know John, class of '48. A fine man."

"I think that's wonderful, Franklin. But you will wait until you graduate?"

"Oh yes, Mother, never fear. I'm not about to do anything rash. Mr. Trowbridge said he can get me into Yale."

And that's all that was said on the subject. Later that day, driving home, Mrs. Denton realized that she hadn't even heard the young girl's name, and she thought that was a bit odd, just that

ALMOST A MAN

Franklin was thinking about "hooking-up" with her. But what did she know? It really was a man's world, say what you like. And Franklin, she guessed, was almost a man, insisting on his Boodles Gin already. Well, she had raised him and what did she know? She supposed Mr. Denton knew what he was doing, and he seemed pleased with this Trowbridge connection. He could put to rest any fears he might have harbored about family slippage. There would almost certainly be a little Franklin Quigly Denton IV, and this one with a line into the Trowbridge clan. She wished she knew the girl's name, though.

PIE

When Mr. Parker returned from lunch, his secretary, Miss Fleming, informed him that there was a man waiting to see him; she winked several times as she conveyed this information; her winks and grimaces were obviously meant to warn Mr. Parker of some aberration in the visitor, or else her face had contracted a degenerative disease overnight, Mr. Parker thought to himself. He glanced around the reception room and quickly located the problem.

"You can have ten minutes of my time," he said to the red-bearded man clutching a tartan cap of some kind.

Taking up their positions in his office, Mr. Parker rested his elbows on his enormous and spotless desk and leaned forward, betraying no emotion. The visitor was busying himself unhitching his backpack and finding a place for it on the floor. He had various colored scarves tied loosely around his neck and in general looked like some tacky Scottish nomad fanatic. Before he had even introduced himself, Mr. Parker felt like he had heard it all before. The man was preoccupied with "settling-in" and oblivious to the ire he had already inspired.

"What is it you would like?" Mr. Parker blurted.

The man stopped fidgeting at last and looked Parker in the eye. "I was wondering if you could help me."

"In what way?"

"Well, let me first tell you something about myself. My name is Brian Delaney and I think I have some ideas, some special gifts, that would help your company."

"In other words, you're looking for a job?"

"Yes, but first let me tell you about myself. I've started seven of my own companies, all of which are still operating today. When my father died several years ago, I divested a considerable fortune he had built on South African gold mines and with that money I started grass roots businesses in depressed communities. And after I did that, I went to live in the woods for a year, like Saint Francis. I meditate, you know. I spent a year in Thailand before that and studied with a Yogi there."

Mr. Parker wanted to strangle this maniac. He also considered firing Miss Fleming for allowing this nut-case to wait for him.

"Would you get to the point," Parker said, barely stifling his urge to scream at the man.

The visitor looked puzzled; he had barely begun his life story.

"Well, yes, where was I? Well, I lived in the woods for a year and felt very close to the birds and squirrels. This was probably due to my deep reading in the early Christian mystics ..."

"I have very little time for this," Mr. Parker injected rudely. "What is it you want from me?"

The visitor shifted his weight back and forth in the chair and ran his fingers through his carrot-colored beard. "But I haven't told you why I am uniquely qualified to be the resident minister of your company."

"Resident minister?" Parker repeated. "We do not have a resident minister ..."

"That's exactly my point. And I think I . . ."

"You want a piece of the pie, is that it?"

"Yes, I would like a piece of the pie," the visitor confessed, somewhat embarrassed to hear himself use such a phrase.

Parker was steaming now. "You sit there in the forest talking to the squirrels for a year, you lie around in Tibet worshipping some bug-infested swami, and now you want to heal the souls of top corporate executives, have I got this right, Mr. . . . Mr. . . . Mr. . . .?"

"Delaney. Well, essentially . . ."

"Well, there is no pie for you, Mr. Delaney. None, do you understand? Now please be so kind as to leave my office. I really do not have time for this."

The visitor began to gather all his baggage and loop it over his arms. He comes begging for a job dressed as if he were about to embark on a long safari, Parker thought. But finally he was gone.

Mr. Parker tried to calm himself. He walked over to the window and stared at the traffic below. Everyone rushing, rushing, rushing to get somewhere. He was tired. He had a right to be tired. He had been rushing all morning. In three more hours he would rush home. He would eat too quickly. Something almost wistful about these thoughts.

Beside his desk a globe of the world sat inert in its oak stand, a gift from his wife, how many years ago? He rarely paid it any attention. He had never twirled it as, he now supposed, she intended. Perhaps now would be a good time.

TRACES OF PLAGUE FOUND NEAR REAGAN RANCH

How can you think of nothing but yourself at a time like this? The Prime Minister is coming on Tuesday. The Deputy Assistant is being held at gunpoint by terrorists demanding the release of a dozen other terrorists, and you want to know if you can go skiing. My God, how have I raised you?"

"I'm sorry father. I know you have a lot on your mind, but I can't do anything about Richard Thayer. Unless you want to exchange me for Mr. Thayer . . ."

"Don't get smart with me, young man. I haven't got time for this. I'm supposed to be at the embassy in twenty minutes and give a statement to the press. Do you have any idea how many reporters will be there from how many countries? And you want to know if you can go skiing. You realize, don't you, that you will have to have security with you? Taxpayers' money. Do you know what the press will have to say about *that*?"

"Father, you don't have to tell anyone. I'm certainly not going to tell anyone. The only people who have to know are Mimi, Rashid and Giselle. I'll use the false I.D. you gave me for my birthday."

"And what about Mimi's mother, you don't think she'll tell all three-hundred women at her club? You're pretty naive for a son of mine. Really, Thomas. I don't know where you've been these past eighteen years, you don't seem to have learned anything. Whether you like it or not, the whole world is watching your every step."

"I'm sure you exaggerate, father. It's true that you are an important man with grave responsibilities, but I on the other hand am merely an average eighteen year old trying to lead a normal life with my girlfriend and a few other friends. I seriously doubt if there is a terrorist in the world who knows my name."

Mr. Crushank's mind was elsewhere by now, and he was busy surveying the contents of his briefcase.

"You tell your mother exactly where you will be at every moment, do you understand? I want it written down, room number, telephone, what name you are registered under. Do you understand? I want to be able to reach you at all times. Do you understand me?"

"Yes, I understand."

"All right, I'm late. Is the driver here? And don't speak loosely with strangers. Do you understand me?"

"I understand. Good luck with the Prime Minister. I hope that goes well."

Mr. Crushank took one last look around the room as though some essential evidence might have escaped his concentration, and then, to his son's relief, he was gone.

It was never a good time to talk with his father about his own ideas or problems. Everything that was his own withered in the shade of his father's world-scale responsibilities. And Thomas knew that his father's pre-occupation with his job was necessary. The world might very well fall apart were it not for a few thousand men like his father, tinkering with codes and messages eighteen hours a day, three-hundred and sixty-five days a year. But then, why do these men have wives and children. Shouldn't they be eunuchs and live in sterilized cells? Why this pretense of pomp and correctness and dinner parties and private schools for children they barely know? When Thomas revealed to his father that he had begun to write poetry, all his father had to say was, "What could you possibly have to say?" And then he paused and thought about it for a moment and added, "When I retire I will write a book. That will be something, I tell you." Thomas was hurt by his father's failure to take him seriously or to allow him one thing that was his own. And Mr. Crushank never thought about it again.

And that was the very first evening that Thomas conceived the idea of running away, of disappearing. He loved his mother, but she was hopelessly tied to this life. She was the perfect mechanical hostess and, increasingly, as the years wore on, she was becoming mechanical in her dealings with her own son. When he was a child she could still let go and roll around with him in the courtyard and call him silly pet names. Now she mostly just repeated her husband's orders and treated Thomas as if he were a negative force on his father's career, a liability on his advancement for which Mr. Crushank had worked with a singlemindedness for more than twenty years.

But just as Thomas was about to accept the indictment of his father and mother, he met Mimi. She could touch that part in him that had never been touched since childhood. She was fresh and alive and he wanted to spend every hour of every day with her. But of course his father disapproved because her father was a lowly speechwriter, and she knew little of the protocol that went with position. His mother did come to his aid, if a bit meekly. "She seems like a very nice girl," was all she had to offer. She did tell a few white lies to cover for Thomas when he was with Mimi.

Thomas dreamed of sneaking back into the States with Mimi and living a quiet life of poverty, a simple life in some state like Vermont, though he barely knew what life was like in the States. He had read *Walden* in school, and this appealed to him, with one major difference: he would share it, everything, with Mimi. "Sell your clothes and keep your thoughts," Thoreau had counseled. But what would his father do, how would his actions be interpreted by the C.I.A., the F.B.I., or, for that matter, the President of the United States himself? He felt twisted and hung on a rack. What would be the advantageous moment to inform his father that he wanted none of it, that he could not go on being a model son, that he was not even vaguely interested in going to college, much less Princeton. Mimi. He wanted Mimi. He wanted to carry water to a chicken, to watch the sun come up. He wanted to work with animals and to eventually have lots of children with Mimi, not just one or two, but five or ten.

As he sat there in his father's study entertaining these delicious thoughts, saying the words *Vermont* and *Mimi* to himself in alternate fashion, his mother was searching for him from room to room in the huge house. When she found him, she was breathless and shaking. "Oh, Thomas, come quick! Your father's been shot. He's at the hospital now. They're operating."

MANSON

One of the children had suggested that the new dog be named Manson. On the first day home from the pound, where they had rescued it from death row, the dog's inclination toward random violence was displayed sufficiently for the name to stick. After dinner Mr. Nelson excused himself and went upstairs with the intention of visiting the lavatory. A terrible ruckus ensued, angry growling followed by cringing cries for help. The children and Mrs. Nelson were laughing so hard at the white terror in his face when he finally made it down the stairs that they neglected to notice that Mr. Nelson's shoes were badly spotted with blood and that his suit trousers were in shreds around his ankles.

"Will one of you kids please go up there and get that dog away from the bathroom door?"

"Daddy," Cindy said, "he won't hurt you. He's just getting used to his new home."

"Look at my cuffs, look at what he did to my trousers. What do you mean he won't bite me? He already has!"

"Oh my," said Mrs. Nelson, "And he broke your skin. I hope he doesn't have rabies." At this the children tittered. A cocker spaniel with such teeth.

"I think I should call the pound and find out if he has had recent rabies shots."

"I just want to go to the lavatory. Will somebody please get that dog away from the door?"

"I'll get him," Timmy volunteered.

"Be careful, Timmy," his mother cautioned.

The Nelsons kept Manson, and grew to love him, although he never really changed. Mrs. Nelson walked him each evening, or rather she lurched and stumbled behind him, herself on a leash, and Manson with the strength of an elephant pulled her through the back streets of the suburban village snarling and growling at any living thing. Neighbors and passers-by soon learned to cross the street at least a half-a-block before passing this loathsome, hateful dog. Mrs. Nelson rarely had the opportunity to explain or apologize as it took all of her energy and concentration to simply avoid being smashed into a tree or a parked car. And yet, she loved him, incorrigible beast that he was.

In the house Manson's territorial imperatives were respected whenever possible. If he was napping on one end of the couch, the entire couch was off-limits to the whole family. If he sprawled in front of the bathroom door the men in the family would relieve themselves in the backyard—a practice that humiliated Mr. Nelson. The women would try to sweet-talk Manson away from the door with promises of his favorite biscuits.

By the end of his first year with the Nelson family, however, all four family members had been sewn up at the hospital, thanks to Manson. One simply never knew when the surprise attack might occur. One night Cindy came home late from a date and tripped over him in the dark. Manson tore at her upper arm savagely and would not let go. The whole family awoke and turned on lights and swatted at the animal with brooms and other long-stemmed instruments until he turned on each of them, releasing Cindy only at the thought of more fresh meat. He quite literally terrorized the entire Nelson family, and yet they loved him. They laughed themselves silly after each incident.

Of course they were no longer able to have house guests or dinner guests or visitors of any kind for fear of injury and lawsuits. Mr. Nelson was adamant about this. He wasn't going to have his modest lifesavings pulled out from under him by some senseless canine felonious attack. Why, even the roof over their heads would be taken away from them should a non-family member suffer the kinds of injuries each of them had experienced. At times they all thought they were insane. They were the fourth family to have rescued Manson from death row. The others had taken him back after a day or two. The Nelsons took some pride in their tolerance and durability, the fact that none of them had actually *died* in Manson's jaws.

Before he had come into their lives there was some question as to who ruled the Nelson household, Mrs. Nelson being a very strong lady herself, and Mr. Nelson known, at least to his children, as an intractable, if respectable old coot. Now there was no question as to who ruled. Manson had established that within minutes, and held without sway the crown and scepter for a full decade, a dramatic and dangerous reign of unpredictable violence that earned him the love and respect of his lowly slaves and peons, collectively known as the Nelson family. It made no sense to anyone who knew of the situation. Friends were lost. Packages were undelivered. The milkman quickly scratched them off his list of customers.

And the more isolated they became, the happier they seemed to be. Tim and Cindy stopped fighting and teasing one another and formed a kind of Manson fan club, they brought him presents and took pictures of him which they had framed and hung on their bedroom walls. Mr. Nelson had never really been comfortable with Mrs. Nelson's dinner parties and was relieved when they stopped of necessity. And Mrs. Nelson got to play Florence Nightingale all the time now, a role she enjoyed, cleaning wounds, applying disinfectants, bandaging. She especially cherished bandaging. They were brought closer together by this cantankerous spaniel with jaws of steel.

One day during Cindy's senior year in high school neither Mr. Nelson nor Mrs. Nelson were feeling well and they asked Cindy if she would mind taking Manson for his walk. Always before they had thought that only themselves were sufficiently responsible and strong to make certain no catastrophe befell their household as a result of these daily outings with Manson. But Cindy convinced her parents that, at eleven years old, Manson no longer had the wherewithal to break her grip on the choke chain and that she was shrewd enough herself to avoid situations that would ignite the devil in old Manson.

But of course she was still only a teenager. The first block went well enough. Twice she had had to distract Manson from his temptation to lunch on smaller dogs running loose in the neighborhood. And once she hid him behind a parked car so that he would not be incited by the sight of the mailman.

Manson dragged her from tree to tree, where he insisted on leaving his mark on each and every one. He even attacked several oaks and actually bit the bark off of them in great anger at something only he could detect, such as the possible existence of other dogs in the universe, a thought which clearly enraged him.

Cindy was panting for her breath when a police car pulled up beside her. The young officer inside reached over and unrolled his window. "Excuse me, young lady," he said, "Could you tell me where . . ." Manson crouched and, with horrendous force, snapped the leash and hurled himself through the air and into the police car window. Cindy lay face down on the sidewalk and heard what sounded like a tremendous explosion. Her knees and elbows were burning with cuts, but she did manage to stand and brush herself off, still dazed. The officer was clutching his face and mumbling to himself over and over and over, "Jesus Christ, Jesus Christ."

"What happened? Are you all right?" Cindy ran over to his window and the officer slowly lowered his hands to reveal a bloody map of Manson's dental charts.

"Oh my God, Oh my God," she couldn't find the words.

The family mourned Manson's death for weeks, for months, really. He was given something of a state funeral in their backyard, one befitting a great dictator. Each of them tossed a red rose into the earth before shoveling the dirt over old Manson's remains. And each had a few words to say about the beast, and all of them, even Mr. Nelson, shed a few tears. An era had passed and, while no one spoke the thought, they knew nothing stood between them and the world now. Their one excuse had been removed, a bullet through his heart. They had their scars and little else to defend themselves against the multifariousness of the world.

MUSH

It was an incredible fight that went on for three days. Frank had thrown all of Stephanie's clothes onto the front lawn. She responded by breaking his favorite pieces of Mayan statuary. He countered by hurling chairs and tables and bookcases through the front door. She bit his ear with all her might, nearly severing part of it. Then she hit him on the head with a tricycle and they made love.

They made love for three days. They did things to one another they had never tried before. He smeared her vagina with his favorite apricot jam. She made a chocolate cast of his penis. It was amazing, worlds opened up to them. Just as he thought he could not possibly achieve another erection, Stephanie had another idea. Frank thought he just might die. Both of their genitals were finally too raw for further use. That's when she suggested that they have another baby. Frank looked forlornly at his withered member and said, "How?"

And that's when Stephanie informed him that she hadn't been using anything during the whole three day orgy. She laughed and laughed at how she had tricked him again. That's how the other three were conceived, after big fights. Because Frank didn't really like children. But then again, neither did Stephanie.

On his way to work the next morning Frank fell asleep at the wheel and narrowly missed a head-on collision with a logging truck. When the driver's horn woke him, not a moment too soon, he almost wished it had been allowed to happen. Each time he had been on the verge of leaving Stephanie she tricked him into staying with another pregnancy. There was never a right moment, she saw to that with her sexual bait. His career as a politician—a city councilman on the rise—no longer mattered to him as it once had before he met Stephanie. He had once said he would be a United States Senator before the age of fifty. That was before he discovered "the mush"—his words—at his core. Stephanie knew about it, and that's what she worked on, Frank's mush.

She liked being married to a city councilman, and she still dreamed, indeed she believed the dream, that he would someday rise above local politics and into national prominence, and she would be there by his side with her brood of little ones. It wasn't the money and all the special perks she wanted but an affirmation that she and Frank were special. Meanwhile it took all the wile and guile she could muster to keep Frank from disappearing into Mexico and losing all trace of him forever, and she knew—though she did not like to acknowledge it in any way—that that was his obsession now. So she was going to make him another baby now. One month later the tests made it official, and Frank was congratulated by everyone in the office. Jokes were made: "Looks good, Senator, father of four, family values. There's no stopping you now." His head was full of obscene panic; he assumed everyone could see the awful mess in there. He even thought of throwing a few of the gawkier ones out of the window or setting fire to his secretary's hair. She knew everything, he was more and more certain. Perhaps she was even to blame, as it was she, Iris, who had introduced him to Stephanie five years back. Yes, Frank was seriously thinking of immolating Iris.

MUSH

Frank treasured the long drives to and from work, forty minutes each way. At the beginning of each drive he had a choice to make: to examine the mush, to rake it over again and again for some clue, some tiny opening out, or to not examine the mush, a much more pleasant choice. If he chose not to examine, he could wake up an old man in Chiapas or Tehuantepec and smell the morning coffee brewing and hear the canaries singing. But then he would be that much further away from actually escaping from Stephanie and the ceaseless caterwauling of the children.

Stephanie greeted him each day with a list of chores it was necessary for him to perform that evening if their common ship was to stay upright and not drift off course. And then she recited all the problems with which she had to contend all day: the babysitter was sick, the washing machine ate three diapers, the plumber had not even bothered to return her calls, her mother had called and was threatening to visit, until Frank thought he was going to explode. He detested domestic trivia, especially Stephanie's, and it was Stephanie's as far as he was concerned, and not his own. He had not asked for any of this. The woman would not be satisfied until she had melted chocolate into his brain and devoured it. How had all this got started? he had asked himself ten thousand times. He could tell the story a thousand ways to himself, but they were all lies. The truth can sometimes be so small and embarrassing, he thought to himself, that it is often not worth mentioning. In this particular case it was tits. He had wanted to suckle from them from the first night she had shown them to him. He had wanted to give up everything and just suckle.

As the birth of the fourth child approached Frank was beginning to make mistakes. Iris was keeping a close eye on him, she was actually keeping a daily diary on his behavior. She justified this by telling herself that she was "covering for him," that is, she was noting mistakes Frank had made, phone calls not returned, conversations that Frank had with various committee members that would have to be smoothed over by her, or by Frank himself if he was still capable. Iris' brother had committed suicide several years back and she knew some of the signs to look for. "Frank is a walking time-bomb" is how she put it to her best friend. "And does his wife, Stephanie, know?" her friend replied. "Stephanie? Are you kidding. Stephanie just wants to be Mrs. Senator. She can't see beyond her big tits." Iris did not usually use that word, but she knew how Stephanie corralled Frank, and she had the burden of her own guilt for introducing Frank to Stephanie. She wished she had made a move on him herself, things would have worked out much better.

When the call actually came from Stephanie saying that she had begun labor, Frank rushed from the office like any expectant husband. But then Stephanie called back again an hour-and-a-half later to ask when Frank had left. And that's when Iris began to worry in earnest.

Mush/not mush. Mush/not mush. Mush/not mush. He raked it over and over all the way home through the traffic, but could no longer even decide which was the choice for today, and he circled and circled the block around their house, trying as hard as he ever had in his life to decide what to think about, *mush or not mush.*

THANKSGIVING: THE RIGHT WAY

She had placed the turkey in the garage two days before Thanksgiving, just as she had for years without any untoward consequence. The crisp, late-November weather was perfect for storage. But something was different this year, something deep and basic had altered the very central fact of her life: her only child, Steven, had left for college, and her husband, Nicholas, had finally moved out and filed for divorce.

And yet, on Thursday, it would still be the three of them at table, Nicholas drinking too much, and Steven, more than likely, stoned on grass, while Anna served the same meal she had for 18 years, inwardly terrified of botching it all for the two most important men in her life. Nicholas's derision could be scalding, she had suffered it for all those years only to discover she was addicted to it. It defined her; in her mind it was all that kept her from disappearing into her own Sargasso Sea. She was still stunned by the divorce. She had assumed he was as crippled by indecisiveness as she, that he would have clung to at least one wonderful memory from the distant past, because no one clung to the past like Anna. She could not let go, she didn't want to let go. And then Nicholas sprung it on her: it was over.

THANKSGIVING: THE RIGHT WAY

What future could there be, with Steven drifting away, and Nicholas filled with contempt for her incompetence, her frightful dependence on him. Oh his terms were generous by almost any standards: she could keep the house, he would pay for all her insurance needs, and of course he would put Steven through college and pay for Steven's car. Beyond that, she was on her own.

He wanted a clean break, as clean as possible. From his point of view, they simply should have never married. He wasn't the marrying kind and he knew this, he knew it from the beginning. The pregnancy had been an accident, and while he loved his son and had worked at being a good father, there was nothing domestic or normal about Nicholas. He came from a large Eastern European immigrant family, and all his brothers and sisters were geniuses or near-geniuses, powerful fanatics of one sort or another. And now Nicholas just wanted to be left alone to find out if anything good might come of his own unruly fanaticism.

And Anna couldn't let go. At least he had given in and agreed to come for Thanksgiving dinner, for Steven, of course. And Anna was trying to make as many dishes as possible ahead of time so there would be fewer opportunities for disaster.

In her fear and caution, disaster sniffed her out. In her trembling insecurity she had planted the seeds for one more cruel humiliation. As she rounded her driveway, home from her little part-time job, she could not believe what she saw: carcass of turkey lay everywhere on the lawn, cranberries scarring the garage floor red, stuffing, green beans splattered here and there, the neighborhood cats and dogs still gnawing on severed wings and drumsticks, blissfully ignorant of the horror gripping her face, the shocked emptiness rising in her throat. All these years, and never before.

She sat in the car, managed to turn off the engine, and started to shake, crying like a hurt child. It was herself, she knew, and not the animals. Though when she finally did get out of the car, she cursed them quietly and made desultory kicks in their direction.

Inside the house, she tried desperately to collect herself. All the walls of the living room still displayed photographs of Nicholas and his mad family. They stared out at her and snapped: "You can't do anything right." She had no strength to fight back; in truth, she never had. She sat now on the well-worn couch and, with a grimly sinking feeling, studied her checkbook balance. It simply was not there. Stare as she might, she did not have fifteen dollars to her name to replace the turkey. She would have to ask Nicholas.

He was drunk and in a foul mood, already filling-up with dread for the requisite feast the next day. And the sight of Anna standing in his doorway inflamed him: Would he never be free of this weak woman!

As she began her wretched tale his face flushed with astonishment. They were both trapped in their own nightmares, and the beast in his must now kill the crippled lamb in hers. Fate had played out its hand.

"My God, woman, is there no end to your stupidity? Can't you get through one day on your own? What did you expect the neighbors' dogs to do, stand guard over it, protect it for you? Jesus Christ and all the gods in heaven, what do you want out of me? Am I to lead you through this life every minute so you won't bump every branch along the road?"

"I'm sorry. I know it was stupid, but it never happened before. Please, just give me the fifteen dollars, I don't want to disturb you."

And after another hour of insults, curses, disparagement of every kind, she got the fifteen dollars, purchased another turkey, and returned to her empty home, to plan the meal again. She would cook her two favorite boys three pies to make up for this bad start. It was going to be a good day, one none of them would ever forget. By God, she was going to get it right this time.

FOLK SONG

From the first outward appearances she was an earthmother. A vegetarian, attentive to her garden, she jogged four miles every morning before 7 a.m. In the summer she wore a ten year old swimsuit that no longer fit. Sweating among the zuks, bulging beyond the cukes, she appeared easy, yearning for recognizable things.

But, in truth, Darcie's mother had committed suicide, and this was something that stood between herself and the rest of the world. She had unconsciously blamed her father, and took little solace from his success in later years.

After an unsuccessful first marriage, Darcie had taken a degree in social work and family counseling. In many ways she lived her life by the code words she learned there, with fond hopes of "bonding" and "coupling" and "parenting." She didn't make new friends but clung fast to her original college-mates, now off in all directions.

After a year or so of living alone and trying to keep up the house and garden by herself, she consciously set forth on a mate-finding expedition. There were plenty of 'types' she knew she didn't want: the "too smart," the "too aggressive," the "too demanding or needy." As the months and years went by, she defined this mate into a honed image, what the exact complement to her life should be.

FOLK SONG

And Johnny was finally it, a 31 year old innocent, living at home with his parents, a good Catholic boy. And Johnny was handy, he liked physical labor, and this fit her needs to a tee. After their first few dates, he jumped right in and was mowing her lawn with zealous dedication. He sawed wood and stacked it for the coming winter. He stripped rotting shingles from her house and pounded on new ones. It was the first time in his life that he felt like a grown-up, like he was coming into his own identity. He would mow long after sunset just to please her.

Darcie didn't really like his friends, or his family for that matter, so they spent most nights alone watching television or listening to the folk music from her college days.

He seemed to pass her tests for compatibility, and they began to discuss the possibility of marriage in the not-too-distant future. Darcie was taking an intense, crash-course at one of the local colleges in order to improve her position at the social agency. It was a time of great stress for her, but then again tolerance for any kind of stress was not her strong suit. She had always said she wanted a family, but when she discovered that she was actually pregnant, a new gloom settled over the household.

Johnny, of course, attributed the mood to the stress caused by the demands on her by schoolwork, and he did everything to help out. After a long day of work for the forestry service, he would hurry home to prepare dinner for her, then start the mower just before sunset and not pause for breath until he could no longer see two feet in front of himself. Then, in the hour or so before retiring to bed, they would discuss the future, which more and more tended toward a recitation of Darcie's fears and complaints. Would the baby be normal? Would Darcie have the strength to continue her job? It took several weeks of this kind of talk before Johnny realized that he was elected to raise the child and that Darcie's depression was not a passing thing.

It was strange for him because, basically, he was a good-natured, uncomplicated fellow. And now, just as he thought his life was taking shape, he had this horrible, sinking feeling. He was caught in a much darker web than he had ever known existed. Darcie trusted nobody, was afraid of almost everything. And the vegetable garden, the folk songs, the talk of having a family, were they simply the leftovers on a dead person's plate?

Darcie insisted that they couldn't marry until she had completed her crash-course, she was under too much pressure, and this complicated matters for Johnny since his family was Catholic. The fact that she was pregnant would be noticeable to all by that time, and, while Johnny could withstand the slight disapproval of several of his family, it still tainted the event for him. Why not a quiet little ceremony now, and then, after the class was finished, invite family and friends to celebrate? She wouldn't hear of it. The marriage would be at the end of the course, and she five months with child.

As that time approached, invitations were sent out, indicating that it would be a potluck reception. Her friends were befuddled by this note of stinginess for it was well-known that her father was a prosperous Florida real estate tycoon who was devoted to his only daughter. But privately Darcie insisted she wouldn't take a cent from him, as though he was responsible for her mother's suicide.

Johnny was realizing that he hadn't seen any of his old pals in months, and that the beginnings of estrangement could be felt with his family. His world had shrunk to Darcie's terrible, but ineffable needs and fears.

At the reception, in Darcie's backyard, his own worst fears were rewarded when Darcie introduced him to her favorite aunt, Molly, her mother's sister. Darcie had talked of her often, with great fondness, and all his hopes sank as he now attempted to talk with her. She was obese, ashen-faced, and incapable of any sort of communication. He reached out to her in his sweetest way, but she recoiled, beyond contact.

Johnny watched Darcie's father now, desperate for some understanding. The father was glad-handing his way through the crowd, a little tight perhaps, but likeable enough. A sixty year old bachelor playboy, it was clear he was a harmless oaf, a bag-of-wind maybe, but he was what he was, and hid his pain at not being allowed to give his daughter away on her wedding day. He made-up for any lack of depth with sheer chatability. Johnny watched him, and thought to himself: this man is not a murderer, he is not guilty, but a victim himself.

The next day, it was business as usual. Darcie complained that she was too tired to go to his family's house for dinner, as they had planned. Johnny was disappointed and embarrassed when he called to make excuses.

In fact, Darcie was tired all the time for months after the wedding. Only once did she summon the energy to go shopping for baby clothes. And then when she returned, Johnny was stunned to find out that she had purchased them all at a Goodwill store, faded, colorless jumpers from another era.

THE DEMONSTRATION

The demonstrators were seated in the middle of the street across from City Hall. They held placards and sang folk songs as they obstructed traffic flow. There were sixty or seventy of them, mostly people with a long history of demonstrating and protesting, professionals. The mood of the group was genial and proud, another moral victory, another notch on their civil disobedience grade-cards.

When the police arrived with their buses for hauling harmless protestors, members of the group handed the officers daisies, and the officers thanked them for their small kindness. The officers were, for the most part, younger than the protestors, and they showed them a certain deference.

"It's a nice day for a demonstration," a baby-faced policeman in dark blue said to a grandmotherly demonstrator with a long braid. "You couldn't have had better weather."

"The papers had predicted rain. I guess we're just lucky," she replied. "I brought a poncho just in case."

"My name is Officer Kearny, and you know we're going to have to arrest you."

"Nice to meet you Officer Kearny. My name is Rosemary Lewis. I know it's your job, don't feel bad about that. And, besides, what good would it do if we just sat here all day and you didn't come and arrest us. We would never get in the papers. We need media coverage if we are to get our message out."

THE DEMONSTRATION

"Oh I understand, I'm very sympathetic with your cause, to tell you the truth. It's just that I always wanted to be a policeman, police work runs in my family."

"I respect that, Officer Kearny. But still I'm afraid you're going to have to drag me onto the bus. It's the way I've always done it, passive resistance, the Gandhi method. He recommends that, and he wrote the book on passive resistance. I hope you don't have a bad back, you're too young for that."

"Well, to tell you the truth, I do have a problem, but I don't want it on my record, so I risk the heavy work when it's necessary, like today."

"I'm sorry to hear that. You should do lots of sit ups and swim. Yes, swimming is the answer for a bad back."

The man sitting next to Mrs. Lewis couldn't help but take in this pleasant exchange. He too was a veteran demonstrator and could rattle off dates and places of two decades of major demonstrations the way others rattle off baseball statistics. Of course he knew many in this crowd today, and he knew everything he needed to know about Rosemary Lewis. She was a notoriously self-righteous and humorless Goody-Two-Shoes who dominated loudspeakers at rallies until somebody had to drag her away, protesting. He disliked her type immensely, preferring instead the singing and the beer and the camaraderie that accompanied a good demonstration, so that when the young officer—young enough to be his son, it occurred to him—bent over and took Mrs. Lewis under the arms, Grover Sheffield, without thinking about it, stood up and grabbed her ankles, and the two men carried the passive lump onto the bus like a sack of flour.

Officer Kearny thanked him and Grover Sheffield took a seat on the bus across from the outraged Mrs. Lewis. She stared straight ahead and fumed, and then finally she couldn't stand it any longer.

"You are a traitor to the cause, Mr. Sheffield. A traitor, that's what you are, and I will tell the reporter at the station."

"Assuming there will be one."

"What?"

"I said, assuming there will be one. Surely there must be more burning business."

"Well! I have never . . . !" Mrs. Lewis's life was demonstrating, and Sheffield's insinuation that today's events had been anything less than heroic got her goat. She had a police record, after all.

As the bus filled up and the singing resumed, the policemen stood around talking among themselves. Grover Sheffield looked out the window at them. He caught Officer Kearny's eye and waved to him to come to his window.

"I hope you didn't hurt your back today. My brother's a back specialist in Brimsville. Here's his card. Tell him I sent you, okay?"

The officer took the card and smiled. "Thanks, mister. I'm sorry we had to arrest you, you seem like a nice group of people. Good luck with your protesting." He seemed embarrassed now and turned and walked away, back to his colleagues in crime-busting.

"Traitor," Mrs. Lewis spat.

"Oh, cork it, Rosemary."

BEEP

There was something faintly amiss with Skip, but I couldn't put my finger on it at first. We'd be driving along in the center of town and for no good reason Skip would roll down the window and yell at some absolute stranger, something innocuous like "Hey!" or "Zow!" Skip is a grown man I should explain. He'd yell these things very loudly and I was, frankly, embarrassed, but I paid little note to it. And the pedestrians, for the most part, just ignored him.

He was in town for a month or so helping me out on a job, so I felt some responsibility for entertaining him. I'd take him out to dinner most nights and he'd talk about his two kids. He was wild about those kids, Jessie and Katrina. Jessie was *the* star of his little league, the way Skip told it, and Katrina could do no wrong. But then, right in the middle of a sentence, his eyes would glaze over, his hands would do a spastic dance over his head, and he would turn to an innocent diner at the next table, and shout some gibberish into their astonished face, "Mutti-mutti-mutti-mutt-mutt!" I was incredibly embarrassed at these odd moments, but had no explanation whatsoever. And the diner, well, he or she often left the restaurant almost immediately.

You can't very well ask somebody directly about this kind of habit. He was a good worker, though, an electrical engineer like myself, and I was taking a liking to him. He called home every night, and then conveyed all the news to me the next day. Jessie, it seemed, was batting 1.000 all summer. And Katrina was picking blueberries and getting to be very compassionate about the plight of migrant workers. His wife Gail sounded like a very special person, too. She missed Skip horribly, she reported each phone call.

I had Skip over to the house on Sundays. We'd have a few beers and play badminton or croquet. He was a tough competitor. But then, out of nowhere, he'd let out some ridiculous howl or bark or squeal—not when we were playing, which might be excused, but when we were just standing around looking at the roses, "mmnmmmunyaaaaaauuu!" and my neighbors would actually open their front doors and look up and down the street, as if the aliens had finally arrived. And again, I had no explanation. In fact, I tried to hide behind a tree on more than one occasion, which is not nice for a grown man.

I was becoming obsessed with this quirk of Skip's. Was it some kind of divine dictation? Or stray cosmic quarks invading his otherwise sane mind? Was he dangerous? He would jump out at me at the oddest moments, contort his face, and say "Beep!" A grown man, an electrical engineer beeping through life randomly. It hurt me, it pained me. I could not for the life of me figure out what was going on. I was on the verge of being afraid, because the continuity of any conversation could break down at any moment into nonsensical animal noises, which is really not fair to the animal world. Skip's voice was sand in the gears of life, grating and, ultimately, destroying the machine by which we live—making sense, cause and response irrelevant. His barks and beeps and whinnies were threatening my equilibrium. And, of course, he was completely oblivious to the serious irritation this little habit of his was causing. He thought we were the best of friends by now. And all I was capable of was x-ing off the days on the calendar, days until his departure: whoopie, yikes, zowie, boom!

"You know, Ray, you've really made this a fun experience for me. I don't know how to thank you. I hope you'll come visit us some time. I'd love for you to meet Gail and the kids. She's quite the cook."

But I was thinking of what it would be like to go through life with a beeper. Or does she beep too? And the kids, little beepers, I suppose. It would be like having a house full of hornets, never knowing when they'd strike, I mean, I've heard of listening to a different drummer, but this one had no beat, no rhythm at all. Or maybe there was a beat and I just wasn't tuned in. I aspired to be generous, so let's just say I'm tone-deaf to Skip's particular melody. He was hearing a tune, the music of insect-angels, methodically stripping our own narrow sense of order and decorum.

As he pulled out of my driveway for the last time I waited for it, for the blat, the burble, the loud vacuity, and when it didn't come I felt cheated, as though he hadn't really said goodbye, he didn't really care. About thirty seconds later I heard it, "Mutta-mutta-mutta-mutt-mutt!" It must have come from two blocks away. Skip was going home. "Beep," I said, "Beep-beep." I was not one whit closer to understanding what any of it meant, but I was going to be keeping a close eye on myself for the next few weeks. I did a little victory dance and bashed my head against the refrigerator a few times. These are dangerous times we live in. Honk.

MY BURDEN

If I had a boat I'd call it ETERNITY and just sail away. But I don't have a boat, I don't have an airplane, I don't have an automobile (that runs), I don't have a motorcycle, I don't have a pony or an elephant or a camel.

With some of the negatives out of the way, here is a list of what I do have: I have a llama (the meanest son-of-a-bitch this side of the Andes mountain range), I have a wagon (needs paint and oil), I have a pocketknife (given to me by my Uncle George when I was six years old). Well, that's enough for now. Already I am beginning to sound pathetic, and I am determined to rise above that.

I would very much like to sell Carl (the llama) to some unsuspecting soul for a thousand or even two thousand dollars. I don't know what he's worth on the open market, as they say. To me he is worth exactly nothing but a pain in the ass. But the only two times I got somebody interested, by taking an ad out in the newspaper, at considerable expense, Carl chased them away with a half-pound spitball fired at a distance of fifteen yards with uncanny accuracy. I can't get close enough to put a muzzle on him, so I'm stuck with the costly, wretched beast. The only way to shear his wool would be to kill him. And I find it impossible to kill him as long as there is any chance in hell of selling him for a thousand or more dollars. You may well ask me how I came to be in possession of Carl, and that is a story I am not fond of telling, because I come out looking like a fool. And nobody hates looking like a fool more than I do.

About five years ago a man by the name of Delbert Monrovia told me he had to go away on business and that he would pay me five dollars a day if I would take in his llama and let him graze in my back yard, see to it that he had a little water now and then, and take him to the vet should he get sick. Well, that sounded like the easiest money a man could earn, just the kind of quick, easy money I always dreamed of making.

Well, in those five years I've had exactly three postcards from this Delbert Monrovia—if that is his real name—and not one cent. And according to my calculations he owes me somewhere in the neighborhood of $9000. Enough money for me to get the hell out of here, which is my sorest ambition. I don't know how long I am expected to wait, but I am losing faith in the good word of this Delbert Monrovia. If that is indeed his real name, then where are his people, I ask you? I have never met or heard of any Monrovias, not that that is conclusive evidence.

I am anxious to join up with my cousin in South Dakota. He is thinking of opening an auto body shop and has more than once insinuated that I could be his partner, if I had something to put into the shop. I think that is a reasonable stipulation. I would not deserve to be called a true partner if I just showed up with nothing but my own two hands, as full of skill as they might be. That is, assuming that my cousin Muscles—that is his true name, Muscles Mulkern—is bringing something to this shop more than his own two hands. Surely he has some considerable savings or why else would he be writing to me about his dream of an auto body shop?

Muscles has been living in a place called Mound City for some years now, and I have every reason to believe that he has established himself there in a manner of comfort and possibly even style. When I knew him as a young boy in Tennessee he had a taste for the finer things in life, in much the way that I now hunger for them. I have no reason to believe we would not be ideal partners in that auto body shop in Mound City, South Dakota, and would quickly be moving in the finer circles. Soon the fine young lads of Mound City would all be working for us, and we would not so much as need to wash our hands at the end of the day before escorting the polite and attractive young ladies of town to the most refined social and cultural events available.

I can see this happening before my eyes if only certain parties would own up to their rightful debts, and I am speaking of you, Mr. Delbert Monrovia, or whoever you really are, gallivanting about, sending me three postcards in over five years. Some people do not deserve the trust and hard work of their servants, for that is what I have been for five long years now, a servant to the ungrateful and spiteful llama, Carl, a beast who is no more mine than the lion in the zoo or the dolphin or giant turtle at the aquarium. I have never wanted a llama, I have no use for a llama, and I have no affection for this particular llama.

So you see it is impossible for me to go away at this time. I have a severe cash-flow problem, thanks to Mr. Delbert Monrovia. While he is enjoying the peripatetic life of the occasional postcard writer, I am tied and bound to this odiferous beast. And

MY BURDEN

Muscles is no doubt at this very moment sketching designs for the name plaque to be hung above the garage outside. He does not even know whether or not to include my name on it, and this is a source of great sadness to me because I have never before had my name on a sign, and just the thought of it makes my heart beat faster, how proud my pappy would be, were he alive to see, that I had finally achieved entrepreneurial status, as he had always dreamed I would. And my dear mama too, she'd be dancing at heaven's gate looking down on her son's name on a sign like that.

Nine-thousand dollars is all I ask of you, Mr. Delbert Monrovia. Carl is as healthy as the day you left. He has never wanted for anything, save perhaps the company of a female llama, which was not within the realm of my responsibility as I saw it. And besides, I do not know of any female llamas in these parts. Whatever your original purpose in acquiring this beast, definitely unnative to this country, I urge you to renew your commitment to that vision, and to relieve me of my watch, with all fair debts settled squarely. Opportunity is truly knocking at my door, and, as my pappy always said, he who hesitates is lost. Mr. Monrovia, I took you for a man of honor. It was your business as to why you chose to own an unnative beast. I did not pry and ask questions that were no business of my own. I simply did what I said I would do. It is high time you do the same. Your honor and your good name—if that is your true name—are hanging in the balance as I survey my future prospects with higher hope and greater determination than heretofore imaginable. Please do not stifle my ambition with your own selfish wanderlust. And if this may help to persuade you to return to your rightful responsibilities, I believe Carl, for all his disagreeableness to others, pines for your special, understanding company, as it was yourself and yourself alone, insofar as I know, who wrenched him from his native climate and, indeed, from his entire extended family kinship, not to mention casual friends, and the very people who have thousands of years of experience with his species, etc., etc., and could anticipate his every wish and need. For these past five years he has had only myself, who never claimed even the most rudimentary knowledge or interest in llamas, and have no inclination to improve my appreciation. I apologize if I repeat myself, but my caring for Carl must cease at the soonest date if my future career prospects are to be kept alive. Great happenings are on the horizon, and time is of the essence. I do hope that your travels have brought you fame and fortune and satisfaction in every regard. If you do not have at least $9000 of it left, then I will certainly be in a pickle in a big way. I only pray that your own mother or father taught you the great virtue of thrift when you were a little boy. My future career, as you know, is riding on this prayer.

THE STOVE

One day there appeared a stove on the lawn of a certain house on our block. A piece of paper was taped to the front of it with the word FREE drawn on it. I walked up the street to examine it more closely. It was a piece of junk about forty years old. I knocked on the screened door. A tiny little woman about ninety-five years of age eventually peeked at me from behind the curtain. Assuming she was deaf, I shouted at her, "Open the door!"

She shouted back, "I'm not deaf!"

"Just take it," she said. "I don't want nothing. Not so much as a cup of coffee." She had a trace of pink lipstick on, but no teeth of any kind.

"It'll cost you ten bucks for me to haul that piece of junk to the dump."

"I don't have ten bucks and if I did you'd be the last numbskull on earth I'd give it to." She started to slam shut the crack she had opened to talk to me.

"Wait a darn minute. Nobody's going to take that thing. It's useless and besides it's an eyesore."

"I want it," a voice behind me said. I nearly fell off the porch with fright. I turned around and there was this stone blind old man, must have been seventy-five if he was a day. He held a white cane and wore wraparound sunglasses and a baseball cap.

THE STOVE

"If it's free I'll take it and I can fix it if it's broken."

"What do you need that stove for? Haven't you got your own stove by now?"

"Sure, I've got my own stove. But if it's free I'll find something to do with it. I'll fix it and then sell it, or give it to some young person just starting out."

"You can have it, blind man," the old lady said, happy to be done with it.

"How in the world do you think you're going to get that thing to your place?" I asked, thinking I had stumped the fool, and that I'd finally get my ten bucks for helping the old lady dispose of the junk in her yard.

"I'll carry it on my back."

The old lady opened the door wider. She was about dead but she still had enough curiosity left in her to want to see what a seventy-five year-old blind man looked like who thought he could carry a stove on his back and not see where he was going.

"Take it," she said. "Just take it and I hope you can sell it for a hundred dollars."

"Okay," I said. "It's yours. And I hope you don't walk off a cliff with it." I paused, for meanness' sake, and because I could hardly think of what to say. "I hope you don't step on a skate or something." I'd never spoken to a blind man before, as well as I could remember. "I hope a rabid dog doesn't chase you down the street." I had exhausted my point.

I said good-bye and good luck to both of them, and as I made my way to go, I heard the old lady say to the blind man, "Blind man, I can't offer you a cup of coffee because I don't have a stove anymore, but if you'd care to step in for a minute I can fix you some lemonade."

I went by two days later to tell her I'd remove the thing for a dollar, but it was gone.

Later, I told my brother-in-law about this. I asked him, "Have you ever heard of a seventy-five year old blind man walking around with a stove on his back?" I was still troubled by this. And my brother-in-law is a pretty smart man because he spent twenty years in prison just thinking.

"It seems obvious to me what happened."

"There's not one thing obvious to me," I said.

"Well, sure it's obvious, you dope. They drank their lemonade. Maybe she had some cookies left over from the last batch she baked before the stove went out on her. Then the blind man offered to fix the stove for her. She guided him as he brought it back in the house. And she thought he was just the greatest guy she'd ever met and told him that he could stay with her, that it would be easier for both of them that way."

"Jesus," I said, "I would have never thought of that. But now that you've pointed this out to me, it makes perfect sense." My brother-in-law truly is a genius of the human heart.

SWEETHAVEN

We had just moved into our rented island beach cottage. Its best feature was the screened-in porch. Boats and yachts of all descriptions sailed right past us. On our part of the island the summer houses are stacked pretty close. It didn't matter; in fact, it was fun to watch the habits of the other vacationers. I've always tried to not judge people, but this guy to our left was making me crazy, fussing all day with his new propane barbecue oven.

It was a real beauty, and he just couldn't take his mind or his hands off it. In the morning, he moved to the back of his cottage. In the afternoon he called to his wife and she helped him lift it up onto their porch. A little later he struggled to pull it down the front steps and set it up on the side of the house. Toward evening he hauled it around in front. Shortly thereafter he pushed it around to the side again. Then he was down on his back playing with the fuel line. I had made up my mind: that big beautiful barbecue oven had my name written all over it.

Toward evening, when he and his wife were enjoying a glass of wine on their porch, I was crawling around under my porch in search of the rusted little hibachi that came with our hut.

I was exhausted by the time he finally fired up his big Cadillac of a barbecue oven. He was far too dainty about the whole process, probably just singeing a little veal. He could have been removing a little girl's appendix when he reached inside to turn over their little morsels. A proper evening of barbecuing, I always thought, should involve large swills of gin or beer, sauce lathered liberally—and therefore messily, a certain amount of cursing and shouting across the yard. But this guy was as clean and quiet as a surgeon, and as smug.

We were renters and they were long-time owners, and therein lies the source of our conflict. They had it all down to a science and we were just groping our way in the dark.

We eventually managed to cook our steaks on our filthy, rusted hibachi. After a beautiful sunset and a couple more glasses of gin, and after the neighbors had turned in for the night—no doubt, with visions of squeaky clean little calves dancing in their heads, I simply strolled over to their yard and lugged their oven over to mine and called Maureen to come help lift the bastard up onto our porch. It was a bold move—and I am no thief—but I simply thought we deserved it as much as anyone. We were paying a fortune for this dingy little cottage.

All Maureen had to say on the subject was, "You're crazy."

"No I'm not," I retorted with absolute confidence.

I think the reason I married Maureen is that she likes crazy. As I said and I repeat, I am not crazy, but if I were, she would not just stick around; I firmly believe that she would love me more.

SWEETHAVEN

Let's call this neighbor Morgan. I think that's his name. On the day following the night of the relocation of Morgan's Cadillac barbecue, he has his Cadillac riding mower out, with equal vigor and ineptitude he is tinkering with every little mechanism. It starts and dies, starts and dies, all morning, all afternoon. His grass doesn't even need mowing, and indeed he never mows a single blade. It's just his habitual holiday routine, perhaps designed—without a thought in his head—to stay out of Mrs. Morgan's hair. Morgan is once again on his back looking up at some faulty mechanism entirely beyond his comprehension, and indeed, this seems to be what he lives for.

All day I'm thinking about what I would really like to have for dinner. After all, we're on vacation. Finally, after many consultations with Maureen, I trot up to the store in town and buy a big slab of pork ribs. Cholesterol be damned, this is a special occasion.

Maureen is making up a load of macaroni salad. Around 7 o'clock the sunset is just kicking-in, and I pour my first tumbler of gin. Morgan, I notice, is about to give up on his riding mower, gazing in wonder into its innards one last time. Another perfect vacation day.

"Hey, Maureen," I yell into the kitchen. "Come help me move the barbecue into the yard."

"But Morgan's still out there, you idiot."

"Never you mind. I've thought this thing through. No problem."

We set it up in front of the porch steps. Right away I fire it up.

I bring the ribs out. I've put on one of those macho men's aprons that say DAD'S ALWAYS RIGHT or some crap. I've got the barbecue sauce, the brush, the poker, everything a genuine barbecue artist must have to create his masterpiece. I even go back in to refill the gin. I'm feeling no pain when I first notice Morgan staring at me from his porch. I even let out a little involuntary "Yippee!"

Then I notice he has gone inside and is standing at his side window looking at me and my beautiful grill through binoculars. His wife is standing beside him and he hands the glasses over to her. The smell of the smoking ribs is ambrosia to my head and I'm swimming in there very happily.

I turn the ribs and slap some more sauce on. I can see Morgan pacing back and forth behind his window, running his hand through his hair, shaking his head.

Finally he comes out and opens the door to his shed beneath his porch. He's in there for three or four minutes. I'm mainly thinking about how long to cook the ribs and how great they're going to taste. This is the first vacation we've been on in several years. Morgan locks the shed and circles his cottage several times. Then he goes back into the house and I can hear his voice nearly breaking.

Maureen comes out with her drink in her hand. "How much longer?" she asks.

"Twenty-five minutes," I tell her.

And that's when Morgan came flying down his steps. He was trying not to run, not to trip and fall, not to make a fool of himself. He was really a decent looking guy, probably sells insurance or something. Maybe a banker.

"Excuse me," he stammers, visibly straining to control his emotions. "Excuse me, but ... but isn't that ... If I'm not mistaken, sir, but ..."

"Take it easy, Jack," I say to him, in my most comforting tone. "Slow down or you'll bust your precious mechanism."

"Now wait a minute," he says, gaining strength. "I believe you are ... I am certain that this is my grill that you are now employing to roast your meat."

His ability to speak the King's English was temporarily out-of-order.

Maureen was cool, serene. She gazed at me with pride and the utmost confidence.

"Chill out, pal," I replied. "This is my barbecue grill as sure as the stars are in heaven. I bought it in East Longmeadow at a True-Value store exactly two months and, let's see, three days ago. Paid $129.95 for it, on sale." I paused to let the incontestable verity of my claim sink in. "However," I went on, "you are welcome to admire its craftsmanship and sculpturesque design."

Maureen was smiling proudly. I looked out toward the sea and added, "That's some view we've got. Come here often?"

"You can't get away with this! You won't get away with this." Morgan was actually shaking his finger at me and quaking.

"A drink would calm you down," Maureen said in her best nurse's voice. "Can I fix you something? A gin and tonic always soothes my nerves when I'm upset over some little nothing."

"This is an outrage," cried Morgan. "What kind of people are you!"

"Well," Maureen began, "I'm mostly Irish, but mother claims I have one-sixteenth Cree Indian in me as well. And Jeff is mostly British with some German blood in there somewhere." I love this woman, especially the one-sixteenth Cree part of her. "And what about yourself, Mr., eh, is it Morgan?"

"You'll hear from me. That's a promise. Common thieves, that's what you are."

"Now there's no reason to be rude," Maureen replied. "Grilling a good slab of pork ribs and watching the sunset isn't a crime, Mr. Morgan. I'm sorry if some misfortune has come your way. Perhaps you need some medical attention, something's out of kilter. I'm sure there's a doctor on the island. I could call . . ."

"Now if you'll pardon us, Mr. Morgan, I have some ribs to finish. Honey, would you mind freshening up my drink?"

Morgan now looks like an insane man, one of those derelicts one finds increasingly walking the streets of big cities talking to themselves. Of course, some of those once held respectable jobs and had families. I don't know what happens to them, something snaps, and they no longer share our experience of the daily world. I can have pity for them but they also frighten me. They're a reminder that it could happen to anyone, including yourself.

"Jeff," Maureen says to me, "I think those babies are about done."

TV

The President of the United States was on the television flapping his wings. He looked like a rooster about to mount a hen who can't stand him. I was looking through my neighbor's window, checking to see if he was still alive. His son had once dropped by my house and asked if I would do this about once a month. Apparently he wasn't on speaking terms with his father, but was more than a little interested in his television set. The old man kept a parakeet, but from what I could see it lacked most of the traditional feathers. I had been looking in on him for about three years and had never seen more than his feet stretched out in front of the stuffed chair from which he watched the soaps and the game shows and whatever else. I was given a number to call if I suspected the end had come.

It was such an undemanding, routine chore to perform that I hadn't really given much thought to the old man, but this one day I was suddenly moved by what I took to be the inert vacuousness of his existence. And his only son never visits to break the tedium or calls to ask if he needs anything. Soon I was hatching a notion that I would pay the old man a visit, maybe try to be, if not his surrogate son, at least something of a friend. Even if all we do is watch some TV together, it would let him know that someone is thinking of him.

I went back home and fixed us a couple of sandwiches, fished out a couple of cans of beer and sodas from the fridge, looked around for what else might perk up his day, some magazines and newspapers, some peppermints. I was a little nervous about this mercy mission, but was committed to following through, perhaps as a down-payment on some future kindness shown to me in my old age.

With my brown sack of offerings clutched at my breast in one arm, I pounded on his door. There was no answer. I pounded again, still no answer. I tried the door. It was locked. I put down my bag and went around the house trying all the windows. They too were locked. I went back to my house and dialed the son's number. His answering machine said, "I can't come to the phone right now, but if you'll leave your name and number I'll get back to you as soon as possible." At the beep I froze, thinking, "This is no way to break the news of the death of someone's parent," and then I thought, "What the hell, this guy will jump for joy, as if he'd won the lottery," and I spoke into the mouthpiece quickly, "Your daddy's bought the farm. You'd better get over here as soon as possible." I hung up and just sat there feeling desolate. I should never have gotten involved in this sordid mess.

Hours went by and no one came. A cloud of gloom sat on my head for the rest of the day and long into the night. I was paralyzed, waiting for the son to show up, wondering if I should call the police.

The next day was Monday and I called in sick to work, I told my boss I had a fever and an upset stomach, must be the flu. A few minutes later I threw up in the sink and then I was so dizzy I had to lie down. I thought to myself, "What if he's been dead for a year, or two years?" And then my mind leapt and thought, "I wonder how much time he has left on his picture-tube warranty?" And I was disgusted with myself for stooping to the low level of the greedy and uncaring son.

Around noon my girlfriend called. She had tried to call me at work and they told her I was home sick.

"Well, I wasn't sick when I called in sick, but then I got sick," I explained to her.

"Why did you call in sick if you weren't sick?" she asked, quite fairly.

"Just come over and I'll explain it all to you," I said. Then added, "There's a dead man in the house next door and I don't know what to do about it."

She arrived about 20 minutes later and I felt better right away. She made me some soup and we sat there talking and smoking cigarettes for awhile.

"The son has got to be some kind of monster," she said.

"I've never even seen the old man," I said.

"Let's just dial 911 and get this over with. You can't skip work another day just to keep this death vigil."

"I know you're right, but I just can't believe the son doesn't care enough to respond at all to his own father's death." Sheila was getting too depressed to keep my depression company.

I leaned over and kissed her. It was meant to be just a comforting kind of kiss, but she responded with pent-up ardor, and the next thing you know we were rolling around on the sofa and then on the floor. She undressed me first, struggling with my jeans and briefs, and then I helped her with her bra and panties, and we made wild love right there on the living room carpet for the next hour or so. I had never known her to be so free and passionate.

"That was beautiful," I said finally.

"The best," she said. "We should do this more often."

I knew what she was thinking: that having a dead person next door reminded one of how good and precious life can be.

As we were getting dressed I noticed someone poking around the old man's house. Sure enough, it was the son at last. He was eating one of the sandwiches I had left on the back stair. What gall! That's it, I thought, I'm going to confront him.

"That's my sandwich he's eating," I said to Sheila. "Can you imagine?"

I ran out the door without waiting for Sheila to finish dressing. "Why didn't you come sooner?" I yelled. "God knows how long he's been dead."

"I was on a fishing trip," he said matter-of-factly. "I didn't get your message until an hour ago. Nice babe, by the way."

"What do you mean by that?" I said.

"I went to your place right away. I couldn't help seeing."

"You what?"

"I could see that you were busy and I just waited until you were finished. You got yourself a real go-getter with that one."

I was incredulous. His father's in there rotting and he's got nothing better to do than window-peep, and then has the gall to tell me.

"Listen, buddy, you're one sick-o character, and I don't want to hear what you think of my girlfriend. The question is, what are you going to do about your father?"

"If he's dead as you say," he paused to take another bite out of my sandwich, "I suppose I'll have him cremated or something. If he's not, I'll just spit in his eye and be gone."

"It's none of my business but if you don't mind telling me what the hell have you got against the poor guy. I mean, you haven't visited him once in the three years I've been looking in on him, as far as I know."

"Well, for one thing, he killed my mother. And, for a second thing, he killed my older brother." Sheila was standing beside me now.

"Why didn't he go to prison?" she asked.

I felt nauseous again and went over to the sack and brought a couple of beers back. I handed one to the son and he cracked it open without so much as a "thanks."

"His lawyer proved it was self-defense. They were trying to kill him in his sleep and it was him or them."

"And where were you when all this was taking place?" Sheila was going to get all this information out of him. That's how she worked.

"I was fishing at the time. I just love to fish, always have."

"And what about the television?" I followed up. "Why do you want that TV so badly?"

"It's just something to have," he said.

He was staring at his beer, in a quiet mood suddenly, and I took the opportunity to look him over, from his shoes to his haircut.

"Sounds like a pretty rough life," I said, maybe intruding where I had no right to go.

"Fishing makes me forget a lot. That's why I go fishing every chance I get."

"But why did they want to kill him?" Sheila asked.

"I don't know," he said. "I suppose it started when he killed our dog."

"And why did he kill your dog?" Sheila asked.

"The dog ate his slippers or something."

"Was he always mean to you? Did he hit you a lot?"

"Not really," he said. "He just liked to watch television in peace with his slippers on." He was still staring at his beer bottle and scratching, almost absentmindedly, some bites he had on his neck. Bites he no doubt sustained while fishing and forgetting his older brother and his mother and his dog and his father.

"You want some dinner?" I asked. "Sheila and I were going to make up lasagna."

He seemed to be thinking about the meaning of "lasagna" for a few long moments.

"That would be great," he said.

I knew he had seen Sheila and me making love just a short time ago, but that seemed like a small thing, like something you would see on TV when real life was tired of you. And the father could wait a bit longer. And, besides, he had wanted his peace above all else. It's amazing what some people will do for a little peace. I guess sometimes "peace" can be the dirtiest word in the English language. "Lasagna," on the other hand, is a very beautiful word.

A CLOUD OF DUST

After several abortions and half a dozen car wrecks, Claire declared she was taking charge of her life. A week later she ran away with an ex-con named Lonnie. Between them they had thirty-two dollars and no friends. Lonnie took amphetamines and drank beer all the way to Texas. He slapped Claire every time she asked him to slow down.

"I don't need you to tell me how to drive, bitch."

"I'm sorry." Lonnie ran over an armadillo and Claire squealed.

"What did I tell you, bitch? You'd have me run off the side of the road to spare a fucking armadillo?"

"I'm sorry, I've never seen an armadillo before, I just wished you could have avoided it."

"You're really something else, you know that? A fucking armadillo. They're pests down here. Get used to it."

Lonnie was driving ninety miles per hour, and Claire could barely see the landscape. She didn't know what she expected to find in this new beginning, but nothing had gone right in her life for years. She was still young, though, and men still made passes at her when she went to bars alone. She had an older brother, but she barely knew where he lived. And her mother thought she was a whore, or so she thought. She hadn't seen her father since she was a little girl. And she hated school the one time she tried it.

A CLOUD OF DUST

"Where are we going to spend the night?" she asked Lonnie as softly as she could.

"You ask too many questions, bitch. We'll stop when I fucking feel like stopping."

Lonnie was darkly handsome, like some of the hoods she had known from a distance when she was still in high school. His menace was a message to the world: Don't tread on me. Claire identified with his anger, though she had never hurt anyone, with the possible exception of her mother, who, she figured, more than deserved to be hurt. Why, she couldn't say.

Lonnie had a gun under the driver's seat. Claire knew he was capable of using it. For Lonnie, other people's lives were not real, they were the straight world which he rejected and despised. The nine-to-five people with their yearly raises and their tidy lawns never got anywhere but older and deeper in debt. He'd show them, the assholes. They thought he was scum, he'd show them.

"Can't we stop for a hamburger soon?" Claire asked.

"You bitches, all you want is food and restrooms. Jesus."

"I didn't have any breakfast, Lonnie. I haven't eaten since last night."

"There's some Fritos on the floor in the back, eat them."

Claire hadn't said goodbye to her mother. Her mother had no idea where she was, probably wouldn't figure out that she had left town for a couple of days. Then what? Claire thought. The police, sure, she would panic and call the police, her little baby has disappeared. What a worrier she was, that woman. Wants to know where her daughter is all the time as if she was a kid still. Always trying to put her on some kind of guilt trip.

A CLOUD OF DUST

When they finally did pull into a drive-in, Claire ordered a foot-long chili-dog and some onion rings. She saw Lonnie check on the gun, and she thought, Christ, not over a lousy three dollars, Lonnie. But then he went up to the counter and fished the money out of his pockets. She watched him pay the girl, the way he eyed her and joked with her. And she thought to herself. I'm already the old lady and I've only been with him one night. They were really in the middle of nowhere, just scrub cactus and sagebrush and no wind and 103° in the shade.

"The girl said there were some cabins for rent another ten miles up the road," Lonnie said when he got back in the car.

"But then what are we going to do?"

"Christ, bitch, how would I know? Get a job, maybe."

"What would be around here?"

"Don't talk so much, okay? You're getting on my nerves."

"It's the pills. I wish you wouldn't take any more."

"Hey, what I do is nobody's business but my own, understand?"

He started the engine and spun gravel as he tore out of the parking lot. The girl behind the counter didn't act surprised. She had seen it all before. They come passing through, running away from something. They want a cabin, a job, some onion-rings. She knew someday she'd just drop her apron and get right in the front seat with a good looking one, stir up a cloud of dust and be gone.

DREAMS OF A ROBOT DANCING BEE

Lately, it seems, my family is obsessed with food, with not having enough of it. We have lived comfortably for years in a middle-class suburb, and now our thoughts have turned to starvation and death, of withering away and disappearing while all around us thrive and multiply.

Jenny, my wife, won a turkey at a raffle last week and it was as though the execution of our family had been temporarily stayed. The kids too acted as though it were the most special gift from God, beyond what they had hoped for in this life. I had to feign happiness for in my heart I knew what it meant: Jenny was the hunter now.

A month from now we will be sucking marrow from the turkey bones. And then we will be eyeing one another carefully. We will listen in our beds at night for who among us will initiate the treachery.

Last night I dreamed again of the deer, tearing his ankles as he punched through the hard crust of the snow. I could feel his spirit weakening, his will to live faltering as the screech of constant pain roared through his body to his brain. There is not much meat on his bones this winter, but I rise from the bed and, still dreaming—I cannot let the dream blow out for one second—I find my boots and parka and penetrate the thick darkness and desolate cold, still holding on to the dream; and it is as though I am following tiny, high-pitched screams, as though I have some kind of radar that is leading me inexorably toward the spot where the deer willingly surrenders his thin, wracked body to me, as though I were performing some act of mercy for which he is grateful. But it is a long journey, and it is excruciatingly cold, and there is some question as to whether or not I can find my way home since the radar is no longer in effect. My son is shrinking before my eyes. He was on the school football team, quite good for a while, but now Jenny has made him quit for fear his bones are too brittle. He is listless and irritable and no longer calls me "Dad." In fact, I don't believe he addresses me directly anymore. He asks his sister to ask me to pass the salt. He was always such a hard worker, mowing lawns in the summer, delivering newspapers, babysitting. Neighbors don't seem to trust him now; they don't like him looking at what they have. They all seem to be doing so well, and John is angry, he doesn't like what he sees. We used to be very close, John and I. I taught him everything I know, and now I don't seem to know anything.

Jenny resents having to work. She was happy being a homemaker. She liked watching her children grow. Now it's my job to stay home and watch them shrink. Missy, my daughter, I love her with all my life, I would lay down my life for her if that would buy her a future of love and allow her to blossom into the beautiful person she should be. But my life buys nothing today and I see the beginnings of a rancid insolence take root in her young body, and she speaks to me with contumely in her once mellifluous voice. Oh my Missy, my Missy, you too are drifting away, away from me, away from the future I wanted for you.

I am a ghost, smoking in the basement, smoking my last cigarette. I am not a part of this home any longer. I am a tiny thing created by indifferent scientists. I am an experiment, a mechanical bee placed near the hive. The real bees were happy being bees until I came along and gave them all the false information that destroyed their little lives.

THE JOURNEY WEST

Babe had been sick for two months, but she wouldn't go to the doctor. She said they were vampires, sucked your blood until not even a miracle could save you. She knew of several cases personally. And she did believe in miracles, though she wasn't religious.

I tried to help out around the house, make her a little dinner, bring her water, make her laugh, I always thought she would get better. And she did too for a while. We made some plans. We planned this big trip out West—Colorado, Wyoming, Montana—driving the back roads, stopping in those dusty, miserable towns. When you don't have to live in them they're great. People look at you like you're crazy to even bother getting out of your car. They look you over to see if you've got anything they might want, or if you offend them. Some of those people take offense real easily. If you've got your hat on at the wrong angle they might want to kill you.

It seems as if I've known Babe my whole life and we've never taken a trip together. She's gone on trips to visit various family members, and I've gone on my own, but we somehow just never got around to taking off together. Which seems too bad because we like the same sorts of things—Prairie Dog Towns, Reptile Gardens, two-headed anything, houses covered with old license plates, good steaks and good bourbon. Well, that's a poor list.

The truth is we're both pretty easy to please. Neither one of us liked shopping malls or big discount stores. I just like her company.

But then she started to let go on me. Regarding the trip, she said one day, "You'll have just as much fun if you go by yourself."

"That's not funny," I said, sterner than I ever meant to sound, "We're going on that trip. You're going to be fine, Babe." I don't know how much I believed either of those statements at that time. I know it took all the strength I had to keep from rolling up into a ball on the floor and crying myself blind. But I didn't want her to see me that way, or any way but strong and reliable, though, in fact, I was coming up shorter and shorter in each of those departments these days.

Babe could barely walk. She could make it to the bathroom and back to bed. But even then sometimes she needed some help. She had dizzy spells, fainting spells. She had a fever most of the time. But it was her eyes that I turned to for the real status report. It seems like such a short time ago I loved their dark, penetrating, feisty, concerned, kindly play. Now I see them saying to me, "Just let me go. It's best if you stop loving me now. It will hurt you less. It will hurt me less. There's nothing more we can do." And I wanted to scream or whisper back to them: "Don't go. You can't go. You can't leave me, you can't leave this world yet. The world won't let you go. Please, please, please!"

"Samantha would go with you," Babe said another time. "You always have a good time with her." She still made these little attempts at humor.

"Can you imagine sitting in a car 10 hours a day with Samantha? Or trying to sleep in a bed beside her? My God, I'd be suicidal or, worse, homicidal by the second day. That woman doesn't know the meaning of silence. I can take her in 2 or 3 hour doses, and even enjoy her wild stories, her nonstop verbal cascades. But at some point I need to escape her presence immediately. I have left her mid-sentence on more occasions than I care to remember."

Babe was laughing, holding her stomach, which I knew caused her very real pain. But sometimes it was worth the pain to let herself laugh.

"Once we get to Hygiene, Wyoming you'll be feeling just fine. I bet they'll have a nice bar there called The Germ Farm or something." Babe had stopped laughing. My jokes had missed their mark. Her eyes had watered up at the thought, I guess, of not sitting at the bar with me in Hygiene. I held her hand tight and tried to smile. I called several doctors who had been recommended to me by various friends and tried to pry diagnoses from them after describing Babe's symptoms as accurately as I could. But there was nothing in it for them except imagined legal suits. I even visited some homeopathy nuts out in the countryside, but their idiocy left me in despair. I called Samantha, who had worked part-time as an E.M.T., an Emergency Medical Technician, and she advised me to make sure Babe drank lots of water and lay still for as long as possible. I felt truly helpless. Babe wouldn't talk on the phone any longer. She didn't open her mail. I paid her bills and watered her plants. We hugged and kissed a lot in the early weeks of her illness, but all that had long since ceased. It was as if our bodies, our senses, had become mere annoyances. I respected her wishes in this regard, but not without enormous pain. Holding her hand or touching her brow occasionally was the sole reminder that we were not already floating in the spirit realm.

Luckily I had accumulated a lot of sick leave days at the Fire Department, where I had worked for more than 10 years. The Chief, Warren Palmer, was pretty understanding. "Sick is sick," was all he said, and I'd try to show up one or two days a week, though often I left early even on those days, beset with worry.

Some days I just sat on a chair beside her bed and we wouldn't say more than a couple of words for fourteen hours or so. I didn't feel ill myself, but I did feel that I was dying, that all that had amused me, engaged me, entertained me and fascinated me for the whole of my life, was no longer of any consequence.

"There's a town called Bar Nunn, in western Wyoming. I don't suppose I could interest you in that? Great antelope steaks, I'm told."

Babe was struggling for breath, and I felt lowlier than a toadstool for even mentioning anything connected to this life. But I felt I had to. I no longer had any interest in taking a trip. I could feel my own level of resignation accelerating. When driving to the store for supplies, it's not that my mind would drift, it would completely shut down. I had no thoughts at all for unknown stretches of time. But then I would come out of it and force myself to practice mental exercises, like picturing Babe before she became ill. I struggle to see her in shorts and a halter bending over in her garden, sitting on the patio with a bottle of beer cracking jokes with friends, or stirring a pot of chili in her kitchen talking to Samantha on the phone. I can't hold on to these images for more than a few precious seconds. They are replaced by darkness, fever, sweat, sheets, bedclothes, rasping noises and then silence. And then a sort of grinding in the earth, which dogs my attempts at sleep.

She wouldn't let me call anyone. And I respected this wish of hers because that was how we had always been with one another. I knew if the shoe were on the other foot she would do the same, even if my request were illegal or weird, she would abide by it.

I sat out on the front stoop one night and tried to count the stars. There weren't that many. It was June and there were a couple of fireflies. I tracked what appeared to be a satellite for a while. The information it gathered, would it help one soul in Hygiene, Wyoming? Would it prolong Babe's life even one moment? I had lived long enough, I had seen what I needed to see. It wasn't bad. It wasn't an ugly mess the way some people said. I smoked a cigarette, savored it, and mentioned to myself that we had probably done the best we could.

Babe had been born in Edwards, Missouri some forty-three years before. And my folks didn't even know where we had come from.

Babe was coughing in the bedroom. It wasn't a normal cough, but something that came up from the depths of creation and turned on itself, and that had its own beauty and righteousness, like certain fires that defy man's best efforts to control them. I was beginning to think that there was another realm where death had its own health plan, its roles for success and prosperity. Babe was no longer just an attractive waitress with a fair share of wit and intelligence, but now she was becoming a CEO of an underground stock exchange where commodities of unimaginable value quietly faded in and out of view. Those of us still living on schedule and following some kind of inept plan would never be able to afford even a glimpse of one share.

I was caught in a dream. "Jack," she said to me, "Let's take off in the morning. I'll get myself together. We'll pack some things. I'll navigate if you'll drive. Those little back roads and shrinking hamlets don't know what they've been missing. Get on your traveling shoes, Jackie, my love, cause we're going to dismantle the West."

CAPTURED

Mr. Roth had chartered a specially equipped ambulance jet to fly his son home after his nearly successful suicide attempt. This was the culmination of years of struggle between father and son. Bernard Roth had married money and gone on with indomitable will to build an empire in construction and real estate. He was used to getting his way. He knew men of power and wealth from coast to coast, but he could not make his only son conform to his ideals. Richard admired his father's drive and his old-fashioned sense of decorum and family honor, but at the same time he wanted different things for himself and had to fight every day of his life for his right to pursue his own interest. And Mr. Roth was hurt and angry at his son's refusal to accept partnership in the family business. There were few souls indeed who did not bend to the iron fist of Bernard Roth's will. *Presidents* asked his advice and yet he could not reach his only son. Nor could Richard ever truly escape his father's long arm. They were locked in a lifelong struggle, where the very real love they could not help but feel for one another was the cruelest weapon of all.

As the private jet touched down on the runway, Mrs. Roth, so small and delicate beside the imposing form of her husband, had to summon great reserves of strength to keep Bernard from collapsing. He was making horrible, involuntary animal sounds as though he were choking and gasping for air. His face, once so supremely confident, was soaked with tears. She had never once in thirty-two years seen him so irrational; control was a virtue he prized among the highest.

"I should have sent him more money, that was it, but I thought he had to learn to make it on his own, I wanted him to become strong, I tried to reach him, I don't know what he wanted, I didn't understand why he chose to live like that, Richard just wouldn't listen to me, I don't know what I should have done, more money, I didn't mind the money, I just wanted him to be strong . . ."

The sight of Richard being unloaded from the jet strapped to the stretcher caused Mr. Roth to quake and tremble until Mrs. Roth insisted that he sit down and breathe deeply.

"You can't blame yourself, father,"—she had never liked the name Bernard and had taken to calling Mr. Roth *father* shortly after Richard's birth—"Richard was always different. It's not your fault. You did everything you could. You offered him a job, you supported him . . ."

Mr. Roth interrupted her impatiently: "We'll get the best neurologist in the country. I'll call the Surgeon General tonight. I've already hired a private nurse, did I tell you? The best. We're going to get that boy back if it takes every cent I've got."

Mrs. Roth already knew her husband would stop at nothing to reverse the hideous damage he had inflicted on himself. Richard had taken a massive overdose of methadone and the first report concluded that he suffered brain death. Mr. Roth's response to those words when they were spoken to him on the long-distance phone call by the resident neurologist had been one of fury laced with threats of punishment. A Roth does not suffer brain death. The incompetent doctor should have his license to practice revoked!

Richard's face was badly discolored, a ghastly purple and black, the result of oxygen deprivation during the thirty-six hours he lay undiscovered. Mr. and Mrs. Roth shuddered and clung to one another, and for a moment the tatter of hope was yanked from their grip and they floated helplessly in the blackness of space with no comfort anywhere in the vast and lonely universe. A team of doctors and nurses scurried about the stretcher adjusting tubes in their son's nostrils and mouth and pushing the I.V. into place and other machines with which the parents were as yet unfamiliar. In all, they were shocked at the sheer tonnage of the machinery it required to keep their son just barely alive. And yet there was not one machine that could arouse him from his deep sleep.

In the weeks and months that followed, Mr. and Mrs. Roth fell into a routine that varied only superficially from day to day. They generally spent eight hours a day at the hospital. Specialists were flown in from the best hospitals in the country. Doctors were replaced several times because of disagreements with Mr. Roth. Setbacks alternated with minor improvements. Infection was finally rooted out of Richard's body, and the low-grade fever that had worried and baffled the team of physicians was finally eradicated. And when Richard opened his eyes some four months after his suicide attempt, the Roth family could not help but rekindle the ashes of their hope. His eyes followed them around the room, and they said things to one another, such as

"He's in there, I just know it, Richard is in there." And they would talk excitedly all through dinner that night, new thoughts, new theories, perhaps a psychologist, perhaps they should ask Richard's friends to make tapes so he could hear their voices, anything that might awaken the brain. There was no way of knowing how much damage was irreversible. Neurologists were cautious, but most of them did not entirely discourage the idea that "miracles" can occur with the brain. It was still a young science, comparatively. And Richard had been an exceptionally intelligent young man. He was special.

In fact, he had become something of a celebrity on the sixth floor of Mt. Sinai. He had a steady stream of visitors, obviously wealthy, important people. And Mr. Roth, while imperious, was also capable of gallantry and generosity when a service has been rendered to his satisfaction. And after his temper had exploded over some imagined or real misdeed, Mrs. Roth was generally there to pick up the pieces and console the wounded victim. Their presence had transformed the intensive care wing into something nearly glamorous.

Richard suffered seizures from time to time, and they were horrible to watch. His face contorted into inexpressible pain, and foam spilled out of the corners of his mouth—his parents were shattered at these times to be of no help at all. Mrs. Roth would bathe his head while Mr. Roth clenched and unclenched his fists and bit his lip. On several of these occasions, the attending physician would force Mr. Roth to accept injections of strong sedatives. They were worried about his health as well. For all his towering force as a man, he was quite visibly deeply shattered. His empire meant little or nothing to him now.

In the evenings Mr. Roth sometimes made long, rambling phone calls to some of Richard's friends around the country. The friends were sympathetic; they knew of Richard's long-standing contest with his father, but none of that seemed to matter now. Mr. Roth was what he was, a broken giant, and they tried to answer most of his questions as honestly as they could, while still protecting him from some of the more unsavory details of Richard's decline.

Mr. Roth at first assumed that all Richard's friends came from wealthy families like himself; and when he was finally disabused of that notion, he felt more confused than ever, and he had to drink himself to sleep, a weakness he would have never tolerated in himself before. Who was Richard Roth? The note Richard had left said simply: *Mom and Dad, I'm sorry. I love you, Richard.*

Mr. and Mrs. Roth considered themselves quite fortunate in their choice of the full-time private nurse they had hired. Angel Montez cared for Richard with single-minded devotion. She even took over some of the duties—such as shaving Richard each morning and washing his hair every other day—that properly belonged to the hospital orderlies. The Roths were moved by her devotion and brought her small gifts of chocolates from time to time. Mr. Roth even presented her with a pair of gold earrings on her birthday.

Angel was very religious and still lived at home with her parents and eight brothers and sisters. Mr. and Mrs. Roth had on several occasions inadvertently interrupted Angel praying at Richard's bedside. She was praying to Jesus on Richard's behalf. Mr. and Mrs. Roth, while they knew this to be unprofessional, were ready to accept help from any quarter.

"Please forgive me, Mr. and Mrs. Roth, I hope I haven't offended you in any way. It's just that I thought . . ."

"That's quite alright, Angel, we understand and we both appreciate all that you have done for Richard, and I know Richard appreciates it too in his own way and would want to thank you if he could. We will all continue to pray in our own way." Mrs. Roth was such a fine lady in Angel's eyes, so kind and strong, and suffering so much pain day after day without once complaining or thinking about herself.

"He smiled at me this morning, Mrs. Roth, I'm certain of it. I was combing his hair, he always likes that, and I was talking to him as I always do, telling him how handsome he looked, and he got this little bitty smile on his face, kind of sweet and devilish, you know. I really think he understands most of what I say to him."

"I know what you mean, Angel. We were here after dinner last night and we were watching one of his favorite Marx Brothers movies, and I'm certain he not only smiled but even chuckled, well, perhaps chuckled is too strong a work, but he made some sort of laughing noises at the right places. I think there's been some kind of growth this week. Mr. Roth thinks so too." Mr. Roth tended to remain silent during these exchanges between Mrs. Roth and Angel. Mexican Catholic women ran heavy traffic in miracles, he knew that.

CAPTURED

"Dr. Wells claims he saw movement in the little finger of Richard's right hand last week, but there's been nothing since. So, while we must keep our hopes alive, we must also remain cautious." He stared out of the window and lit a cigarette. He had never smoked before this tragedy visited their lives, and he disapproved of it thoroughly.

"Has Dr. Somerset been in today?" he asked Angel.

"No, I think he is in surgery this morning."

"Goddamn these doctors! I pay them a fortune and they are never here."

Angel still winced automatically at Mr. Roth's frequent sacrilegious profanity, but she was getting accustomed to it. Still, she knew he was a gentleman in every other way and was gravely distraught at his only son's miniscule progress. So she forgave him this little sin.

At home she talked to her mother and her sisters about Richard and about Mr. and Mrs. Roth. Mrs. Montez did not even act surprised when Angel confessed to her one day that she thought Richard might some day ask her to marry him. Mrs. Montez saw her daughter's devotion to this fine, young man, as ill as he might be, to be a sure sign of her daughter's religious and charitable nature, and this was good. For her good deeds in this world she may some day be a saint. That's how she thought about it as she stirred a big fish soup.

It was only a few days after Angel had confessed her secret thoughts to her mother that a nearly miraculous thing happened. Angel had arrived at the hospital early and was alone in the room with Richard, talking to him as usual. Her manner might be described as coquettish or flirtatious when she was alone with him, but it was all very sweet and innocent. She batted her eyelids at him when she puffed up his pillow or straightened his sheets. She chatted on to him as if he were a soldier back from the front with a shoulder wound.

"I have a surprise for you today, " she said to him. And then it happened, the miracle.

Barely audible, so that she had to wonder, much later, if she had made it up herself, he said "Wha . . ."

Merciful Mary, she thought, he spoke! Richard spoke! He spoke to me! At which point she neglected to answer, she forgot to show him the little friendship ring she had bought for him with the engraved message inside that read simply *Love Angel.* She was dizzy with excitement and needed to tell somebody, everybody, the news of the miracle. His first word in six months and it was to her!

She raced down the corridor and frightened Julie, the nurse at the head desk, with her manic reconstruction of the incident.

Julie was slow to respond, to join Angel in her unbound joy, and instead advised her to pass on her little story to Dr. Somerset when he comes in in an hour or so. Angel looked around the corridor for someone, anyone now, who could understand the significance of what had just happened, and that is when, God sent, Mr. and Mrs. Roth came walking through the big double doors at the end of the hall.

It was another long and emotionally draining day for Richard's parents. Richard had suffered another seizure around eleven o'clock, and the inevitable setback had left him nearly lifeless through the rest of the afternoon. The Roths had finally left for a restaurant around 6:30. Mr. Roth stared into his second cocktail in silence for minutes at a time, and Mrs. Roth respected his silence.

"She's a dangerous woman," he said finally.

"Who?" Mrs. Roth had no idea of whom he was speaking.
"Angel. We'll have to replace her."

"But, Father, what are you saying? No one could be more selfless in their devotion to Richard." Mrs. Roth was never to contradict her husband. But she too was exhausted now and couldn't comprehend her husband's desire to hurt such a good person, such an exemplary private nurse.

"I will not have my emotions toyed with by this Bible-beating beano wench."

The subject was dropped, but Mrs. Roth was afraid for them, afraid of what they might become, she and her husband, in their endless and helpless grief.

Angel told her mother of the miracle, though some of the joy had been dampened by Richard's subsequent setback. Her mother wasn't certain if it qualified as a miracle, but she promised to ask the priest that week.

DEWEY'S SONG

Benton Snead's nephew, Dewey, slept all day in a broken-down Plymouth Falcon in the backyard. He hung rags over the windows to keep the sun out. Benton went about his work in the yard as if Dewey didn't exist. Indeed, Mr. Snead wished he existed some place far away where he would never have to see him again, some place like, say, Pluto. Dewey was unemployable, he was un-everything as far as Benton Snead was concerned.

Dewey had his own routine. He would rise from sleep around seven in the evening. Then there followed a five mile walk to the shopping mall where he would perform his ablutions in the public toilet. Innocent intruders were often puzzled by Dewey's public bathing, and Dewey encouraged shoppers to believe it was his own private facility, then he would generously offer to share it with them, perhaps for a small token of gratitude. Then Dewey would take his only meal of the day at one of the greasy spoons that line the highway leading to the mall.

In short, Dewey lived out his days without conversation or social exchange. Benton Snead was embarrassed whenever a neighbor referred to seeing Dewey making his rounds. Dewey had been dumped on him by his sister who had banned him from her own house. Mr. Snead lived alone his whole life, a bachelor who loved his garden more than anything. Periodically, he would strike a deal with Dewey, but it was always a mistake.

"You paint the house, and paint it right, and I'll let you

sleep in the attic for awhile. No messing around, do you understand?"

Dewey was picking flakes of yellowed newspaper out of his hair.

"Do you hear me, you dag-blamed idiot?"

"Uncle Benton, I don't mind the car. It suits me just fine."

But Mr. Snead really did want his house painted, and he was too old to do it himself now. Last time he tried to paint it himself he fell off the ladder and had his shoulder in a cast for two months. And he was too cheap to pay anyone else to do it.

"Do you want to do it or not, you lazy good-for-nothing?"

Dewey never wanted to do anything, but sing. He sang in the church choir on Sundays and to everyone's amazement, he sang like an angel.

"I don't know much about painting houses, Uncle Benton."

"Crime-in-Itly, boy, I'll show you how to paint it. Any idiot can paint a house."

And, much to the amusement of Mr. Snead's neighbors, Dewey proceeded to paint his uncle's house at night. The daft young man would shine the lights of the defunct Falcon onto the side of the house and paint. Should anyone awake at two or three in the morning, there he would be, a ghostly dream on a ladder. Benton Snead was disgusted but could do nothing about it. Dewey still preferred the washroom at the mall to his uncle's. His routine varied almost not at all, even with a roof over his head. Dewey was incorrigible. Mr. Snead had given up hoping that the Army would take his nephew, or that some unfortunate, lame-brained woman would take him off his hands. He was going to die with this whacko nephew tied around his neck.

DEWEY'S SONG

Dewey finished painting the house, but of course there were large splotches he missed altogether, painting in that eerie light. But Mr. Snead grudgingly thanked Dewey anyway, since it was about the only thing he had ever stuck with in his whole life, except the singing. The two men walked around the house and admired those parts Dewey had covered.

"Not too bad, considering your approach."

Dewey was all smiles, he wasn't dumb. He wasn't dumb at all. He just didn't want what most people wanted.

"I'm going to London next week, Uncle. I thought I should tell you. I've got a job singing. Reverend Starkey recommended me. I tried out last Sunday and I got word today. They're paying for my ticket and everything."

Mr. Snead was stunned. "You've got to be kidding me, somebody's flying you to London just so you can sing for 'em?"

"That's right, Uncle Benton. I'm going to be singing seven days a week."

"But how . . . What . . ."

"You've been real good to me, Uncle Benton. My mother always said I would amount to nothing. You tell her for me, will you?"

"But Dewey, what if something happens to me? What if I have a heart attack mowing the lawn? What if I have a stroke picking beans?"

Dewey looked his uncle in the face and saw how afraid he was of dying alone.

"I'll sing at your funeral, Uncle Benton. You'll hear me because I'll sing prettier than I ever sung in my whole life. You'll see, it won't be so bad."

FAREWELL, I LOVE YOU, AND GOODBYE

Our lives go on. Our fathers die. Our daughters run away. Our wives leave us. And still we go on. Occasionally we are forced (or so we like to say) to sell everything and move on, start over. We are fond of this myth mainly because we have so few left. The Starting-Over-God is, of course, as arbitrary as the one who took father before his time. But we have to hang onto something. So we start over. There is a little excitement to spice the enormous dread. Not again, I can't, I don't have it in me. I've seen this one before and I can't sit through it again. But we do, just in case. In case we missed some tiny but delicious detail all the other times we saw it.

Can you recommend a dentist, a doctor, an accountant, a reliable real estate agent, a bank? And before you know it, a life is beginning to fall into place. You have located the best dry cleaner, the best Chinese food. A couple of the shop owners have remembered your name. How long have you been here? they ask. And here is the opening, the opportunity you've been waiting for.

"I was born here," you reply, "lived here all my life." Rooms full of pain, lawns of remorse, avenues of regret, whole shopping malls of grief begin to detach themselves from you, from the person, from this husk, this shell you call simply Bill.

"My name's Bill, I live just down the street, it's funny we haven't met before."

"Nice to meet you Bill. My name's Carla. I just opened the shop a week ago. I moved here from Chicago last summer. Divorce, you know."

She was an attractive woman, slight, fine-boned, and had a pleasant manner, and Bill couldn't imagine why anyone ... He stopped himself. Let it go, let her previous life go. And why had he lied to her automatically? He wanted to clear it up right away, but what would she think, telling lies to a stranger, what kind of behavior is that, anyway?

"Carla, I have to apologize to you."

"Why? I don't understand."

"I haven't lived here all my life. I'm new in town. I just ..."

"That's all right, you don't have to say anything."

"Well, then, can I buy you a drink or something when you close up today or some other day?"

"That'd be nice. Can you come by about five past five?"

"Great." And so, it was starting again. Some single-minded agent of life was stirring, was raising its perky head, and Bill smiled and waved goodbye to Carla.

On the short walk back to his house Bill found himself humming an old Billy Holiday tune, "God Bless the Child that's got his own," and he laughed at himself and shook his head. Here he was in his new place, his new life, so much blood and ashes under the bridge. But it wasn't under the bridge. It was *his*, all that pain was not washed away, it was his, and suddenly he was proud of that. *Carla*, he said the name several times out loud. *Carla*, wow, who would have thought.